"You're not listening to me!"

"Sure I am, darlin'. Yer afraid all this sneezin' and coughin' is gonna be a bother to me once we're married, is that right?"

"Yes," she said, her voice barely above a whisper. "I am."

"Well, I'll tell ya right now, I ain't worried 'bout it. I know sure as the sun sets that Ma'll figure somethin' out. She always does."

Ebba sighed heavily...and felt her nose start to tickle. *Here it comes...*

"Look at me, sweetie," Daniel instructed.

Ebba looked into his eyes, gasped at the tenderness in them...and sneezed.

"Ya know what?" he asked gently.

She sneezed again, though thankfully she had time to turn her head first. "What?" she asked miserably.

"I think we're gonna get along just fine."

Kit Morgan has written all her life. Her whimsical stories are fun, inspirational, sweet and clean, and depict a strong sense of family and community. She was raised by a homicide detective, so one would think she'd write suspense, but no. Kit likes fun and romantic Westerns! Kit resides in the beautiful Pacific Northwest in a little log cabin on Clear Creek, after which her fictional town that appears in many of her books is named.

DEAR MR. WEAVER

KIT MORGAN

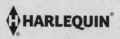

ISBN-13: 978-1-335-47408-7

Dear Mr. Weaver

First published in 2016 by Angel Creek Press.
This edition published in 2020.

Copyright © 2016 by Kit Morgan

Recycling programs
for this product may
not exist in your area.

This edition published by arrangement with Harlequin Books S.A.

For questions and comments about the quality of this book, please contact us at CustomerService@Harlequin.com.

Harlequin Enterprises ULC
22 Adelaide St. West, 40th Floor
Toronto, Ontario M5H 4E3, Canada
www.Harlequin.com

Printed in U.S.A.

Chapter One

Denver, Colorado,
1901

Fantine LeBlanc sat nervously and waited as Adelia Pettigrew read her application.

She'd been sent to the woman by the employment agency and been warned that Mrs. Pettigrew was a tad…eccentric. She tried not to fidget as the woman casually perused her résumé through a diamond-studded monocle pinned to her dress with a silver chain. That wasn't anything unusual. It was the thin cigar the woman was smoking that had Fantine's heart racing—and her lungs coughing.

Mrs. Pettigrew looked up from the paper in hand. "What is this? Do you need some water, *ma petite*?"

"No, *Madame* Pettigrew, I am fine," she answered in her delicate French accent. Mrs. Pettigrew, on the other hand, sounded like a Frenchwoman trying to speak like an American Southerner. Or was it the other way around? Fantine wasn't sure.

Mrs. Pettigrew took another drag of her cigar and blew the smoke at her. "I think you should have some water, *ma petite*. You look ill."

Fantine coughed again and waved the smoke from her face. "If you insist," she rasped.

Mrs. Pettigrew got up, went to a small sideboard laden with glasses, a water pitcher and several decanters of who only knew what, and poured a glass of water. She crossed the room and handed it to her. "Here, this will help. You must be catching cold."

Fantine half-smile and nodded. "I must." She took the glass and drank, then set it on the desk.

Mrs. Pettigrew re-took her seat. "I see you speak several languages," she remarked, looking at the paper again. "That will be useful. One never knows where a bride may originate from."

Fantine glanced around the room. Every square inch of the walls was covered with picture frames holding what looked like letters. "You have sent out many brides over the years, haven't you, *Madame*?"

Mrs. Pettigrew leaned back and waved a hand in the air. "More than I can count at this point. After twenty-five years in business, who can keep track?"

"And what about all of these?" Fantine motioned toward the nearest wall.

"Those? They are letters from some of my favorite customers. I try to keep in contact with all my brides after sending them off to be wed, but these…" She pointed at the walls with both hands. "…these are my triumphs!"

"Triumphs, *Madame*?"

"*Oui*, for these letters are from brides who never thought they'd make it with their new husbands. They wanted to give up before their adventures even started! They all wrote to me, told me of their woes and how they wished to return, but no! I would not let them."

Fantine stared at the woman. She was taller than most, with raven-black hair streaked grey at the temples. She had the most beautiful blue eyes and a complexion to die for, at least for someone her age. The woman had to be in her fifties, but still had the look of one much younger. Rumor had it that she was wealthy, the widow of a miner who'd struck it rich near Cripple Creek back in the 1860s. The Pettigrews had built an empire together, but now only Mrs. Pettigrew remained to enjoy it. "Why do you help women become mail-order brides?"

"Why?" Mrs. Pettigrew said as if insulted. "Because someone has to help the women of this town find happiness! I have had mine, and have always believed I could help others find theirs too."

"But why as mail-order brides?"

"Because of the adventure, what else?"

Fantine's nose twitched, a nervous tic. Maybe she should become a mail-order bride instead of applying for the position of personal assistant to this madwoman. "Did any of them ever come back?"

"*Sacre bleu*, of course not! Not one of my brides has ever returned to Denver, except on a visit to show off their husband. Granted, I have not always been in Denver, but even before, I've always had satisfied customers."

"I meant no disrespect, *Madame*. I...was just curious. Which makes me want to ask, where did you begin if not here in Denver?"

Mrs. Pettigrew sighed. "Well now, *ma cherie*, that is a story." She smiled. "A very long one—too long for today, I'm afraid." She got up, went to the far wall and took down one picture frame, bringing it to the desk and setting it before Fantine. "This was my first...for Denver, that is."

Fantine picked up the frame and studied the letter. It was dated June 8, 1876. "This is over twenty years old."

"Yes and Ebba is doing wonderfully."

"You still hear from this woman?" Fantine asked in disbelief.

"But of course. I hear from many of my girls to this day."

Fantine stared at her with wide eyes before she let them drift to the framed letter and began to read.

Dear Mrs. Pettigrew,
I've reached my destination and I must say that the Washington Territory is not what I expected. Neither is my new husband, for that matter. His family is huge, loud and boisterous! We haven't had a moment's peace since my arrival. I don't mean to complain, but I wasn't prepared to become a schoolteacher for seven children—seven mischievous, prank-pulling children, no less. No,

they are not my husband's (thank Heaven). They belong to his older brother and his wife. I should have been warned! He said nothing in his letters about any of this. I don't know how much longer I can endure it. Please write back to me as soon as you can before I go mad!
Sincerely,
Ebba Weaver

Fantine raised her eyes to Mrs. Pettigrew's. "What happened?"

"Oh, my dear sweet child," she said with a roll of her own eyes. "What *didn't* happen is a better question."

Fantine scooted to the edge of her chair. "How so?"

Mrs. Pettigrew chuckled. "Well, I suppose I can tell you a little. Ebba Knudsen came to me on a spring day, much like this one. I had just opened this bridal agency, back when Colorado was still a territory. It became a state later that year. But what does that matter? What does is where I sent Miss Knudsen."

"Where did you send her?"

"To a little town called Nowhere, in what was the Washington Territory."

"Nowhere? Who names a town Nowhere?"

Mrs. Pettigrew shrugged. "Who knows? But that is where I sent Ebba."

"What happened to her?"

Mrs. Pettigrew leaned forward. "She married a *Weaver.*"

"A clothmaker?"

"No, no—not a weaver, but a man named Weaver,

from a large family of Weavers! A man of many talents, but also of many brothers and cousins and nieces and nephews…well, you understand now, I think."

Fantine settled herself more comfortably in her chair. "And he didn't tell Miss Knudsen about them?"

Mrs. Pettigrew looked at the ceiling in thought. "Not that I recall, no."

"What do you recall, *Madame*?"

Mrs. Pettigrew smiled. "Well, let me see…"

Denver, Colorado Territory,
April 10, 1876

Ebba Knudsen stood as the owner of Pettigrew's Bridal Agency walked a slow circle around her. "Chin up, don't slouch," the woman ordered. "You want your future husband to be proud of his new wife, not cringe at your stooped shoulders."

Ebba swallowed hard. Maybe this wasn't such a good idea. What made her think she could become a mail-order bride? Obviously there was a lot more to it than she first thought: pick a prospective husband from a stack of applicants, write a few letters, receive some train fare and off you go. But what did she know?

"*Mademoiselle* Knudsen! Are you listening?"

Ebba snapped to attention. "Yes, ma'am," she answered with a Swedish accent.

Mrs. Pettigrew's eyes grew wide. She pulled a monocle from her skirt pocket, put it over one eye and peered at Ebba as if inspecting an odd insect. "Come again?"

Ebba curtsied, unsure of what the woman wanted. "I said yes, ma'am."

Mrs. Pettigrew let the monocle fall from her eye into her waiting hand. "That's what I thought you said." She looked her up and down. "You didn't tell me you were Swedish."

"I saw no reason to."

"And you'd be quite right." Mrs. Pettigrew studied her. "Your hair is too dark, for a blonde that is, your eyes…" She placed the monocle over her eye again. "…Well, I suppose green will have to do. I was expecting a deep blue considering your heritage. But you do have nice cheekbones…"

"Is that relevant?" Ebba blurted.

Mrs. Pettigrew looked at her aghast. "It most certainly is, *ma petite*! How else will I match you with the most perfect gentleman possible?"

Ebba opened her mouth to speak, but couldn't come up with anything to say to that other than "Oh."

"Qualifications?"

Ebba shook herself. "I beg your pardon?"

"What qualifies you to be a wife?" Mrs. Pettigrew walked behind her desk and sat.

Ebba felt her throat tighten. "Qualify?"

"But of course! I don't send off just any mail-order brides. I send off the finest."

Ebba swallowed hard. This was definitely not a good idea—she might as well turn around and march right out the door. Maybe slaving over other people's laundry wouldn't be so bad…for the rest of her life…until the day she died…oh dear.

"Can you cook?"

Ebba shivered at the question, her mind still on a life full of dirty laundry. "Er...yes."

"Good. Sew?"

"Yes, I sew very well." Well enough to be hired on by Mrs. Feldnick as a laundress. Though her sewing skills were wasted there—laundry was the order of the day and lots of it.

"Are you organized?"

"What?"

"Organized? Can you clean a house from top to bottom? Make it shipshape?"

Ebba rubbed her temples. "Yes." Maybe if she left now, the woman wouldn't be too upset.

"I have just the applicant."

Ebba's hands dropped to her sides. "You do?" she said in shock.

"Yes, I think he'll be perfect for you. Tell me, do you like the country?"

Ebba's heart began to beat like a thundering herd of horses. "Well..."

"The open air? The smell of fields? Oh, but you'll love being a farmer's wife!"

Ebba gulped. She'd been born and raised in New York City, lived in Chicago for a time and had only recently moved to Denver with her parents. Both of which, unfortunately, were now dead. "Farmer's wife?"

"He writes in his preliminary letter that Nowhere grows some of the best apples in the world!"

"Apples." She was still back at the part about being a farmer's wife. "Perhaps a shopkeeper, or a banker or merchant, would be a better match, *ja*?" Under stress, her Swedish slipped out.

"None of those will do. A farmer will be perfect!"

Ebba's shoulders slumped again. She had no idea how to be a farmer's wife. But then, what other type of man sent away for a mail-order bride? A banker certainly wouldn't—there would be no need unless the area in which he lived was completely bereft of eligible women. But a farmer might live well out of town somewhere, which meant animals and fields and barns and…sneezing. Lots and lots of sneezing!

Ebba eyes watered at the thought and her nose twitched. She couldn't possibly! "Mrs. Pettigrew, I don't think this man would be a good match at all."

Mrs. Pettigrew tapped a few papers on her desk to straighten them. "He's perfect."

"No…he's not," she stammered and took a step toward the desk. "He would be all wrong…"

"You *can* read and write, can't you?" the woman asked suspiciously.

"Yes, of course, but…"

"Oh, thank goodness. This man stipulates he must have a wife who can read and write." She glanced up from the paper in her hand. "Then what is the problem? At least one of you will be able to."

A chill went up Ebba's spine. "*One* of us?" she squeaked. "Oh dear…" She glanced around for someplace to sit, spotted a chair a few steps away and went to it. "I need to think."

"What is there to think about?" Mrs. Pettigrew asked in shock. "I grant you, men like this often have someone else answer the advertisement for a bride, as they haven't the necessary skills. But as long as you can read... I have a wonderful man waiting for a wonderful wife! Are you saying you are not wonderful?"

"No! That's not what I'm saying at all—"

"Good, sign here." Mrs. Pettigrew shoved a paper across the desk. She dipped a pen into an inkwell, held it out and waited for Ebba to take it.

Ebba stared at it as if it were some poisonous snake.

"Come now, Miss Knudsen. It will be the adventure of a lifetime."

Adventure, yes, but all Ebba could think about was her allergies. Sneezing, coughing, itchy eyes, the constant tickle in her throat... "Have you any other applicants? One that lives by the sea, perhaps?" She'd heard that the seacoast was wonderful for her particular malady.

Mrs. Pettigrew frowned. "I'm afraid not. Mr. Weaver is the best applicant I have for you at the moment. Unless you'd like to wait?"

Ebba paled. To wait meant becoming a slave to Mrs. Feldnick for who knew how long. "No, I can't wait." She pulled the paper the rest of the way, took the pen and signed. She shoved it back across the desk. "Now what do I do?"

"Write him back, of course, and tell him you accept his proposal."

"What proposal? The man hasn't proposed. I've seen nothing from him. Isn't there supposed to be a letter or something I'm to read?"

"Oh yes, of course, of course..." Mrs. Pettigrew

pulled out another sheet of paper from a pile in front of her. "Here it is."

Ebba took it from her and read:

My Dearest Bride,
My name is Daniel Weaver, and I am writing to you because I want to marry you. I'm tall with dark hair and green eyes. My mother tells me they are my best feature. I work on a farm outside the town of Nowhere in the Washington Territory. I was born and raised here, and there is no place on Earth like it. Now that I am of marriageable age (24) I am ready to take on a wife to help me farm. We raise apples, pears, walnuts, and keep cattle, sheep, and chickens. The farm is a wonderful place and I cannot wait to marry and raise a family. I am a strong man and love working the beautiful land the good Lord has provided. This means I can provide for you too. My dream is to marry a woman to work alongside me in my peaceful slice of Heaven. I hope to see you soon.
Yours truly,
Daniel Weaver

Ebba looked up from the letter. "He says 'we.' What 'we' is he talking about?"

"Perhaps his mother?" Mrs. Pettigrew suggested. "Since he mentions her in the letter, who else could it be? You would then have another woman in the house to talk to."

Ebba absently nodded. "Yes, I suppose."

"Ah, a quiet country life! I always dreamt of such a thing, to live in the French countryside on a lovely little farm…but alas, it was not to be."

Ebba noted the faraway look on her face and grimaced. "You *wanted* to live on a farm?"

"But of course, *ma petite*. Who wouldn't want a peaceful life in the country? But my work is here, and it is here where I can do the most good."

"Good?"

"Of course, by helping young women like yourself find good husbands. It is my true joy!"

Ebba smiled half-heartedly. Mrs. Pettigrew had a reputation for being an odd duck. But she was also supposed to be a superb matchmaker, be it through her mail-order bride agency or otherwise. Which made Ebba wonder. "Why aren't you married?"

Mrs. Pettigrew put a hand to her chest and sighed. "I was, *ma belle*, I was—to a wonderful man. But he died." She hung her head. "However, he did leave me a considerable fortune, one that makes it possible for me to do what I am best at. Matchmaking!"

That made sense. Ebba and her parents had heard about the Pettigrew fortune not long after coming to Denver. But it wasn't Mrs. Pettigrew's money that so often had her in the social gossip pages—it was her eccentric behavior, and speculation about her past. Though no one seemed to know what that past consisted of. "I put my trust in your good judgment, Mrs. Pettigrew."

"Of course you do! Now you must write the young gentleman back!" She opened a drawer of the desk, pulled out a sheet of paper, then shoved it and the pen and inkwell at her. "Go ahead, don't take long."

"What do I tell him?"

"About yourself, of course! Your skills, your pretty eyes and hair, your wonderful figure…well, perhaps not that. He will see for himself, *oui*?"

Ebba grimaced again. Yes, she knew she wasn't hard to look at, but would her future groom think so when she was red-faced and sneezing? And yet, what other choice did she have but to risk it? She picked up the pen, dipped it into the ink and started to write.

Chapter Two

Dear Mr. Weaver:

My name is Ebba Knudsen. Mrs. Pettigrew of the Pettigrew Bridal Agency has assured me that you would make a good match. Let me tell you a little about myself and you can be the judge.

I am twenty years old. My parents came to America from Sweden, and our family moved to Denver from Chicago about a year ago because their doctor thought the air here would be good for them. Alas, they are now dead. Because of this, I have decided to become a mail-order bride. Mrs. Pettigrew comes highly recommended, so I sought her help.

I am five feet and three inches tall with blonde hair and green eyes. I am a hard worker and would keep your house clean and can sew for you. I am a fair cook, though my parents thought I was excellent. I learned to cook from both my mother and my mormor (Swedish for grand-

mother). I have no brothers or sisters and no family left to me in this country. I don't like being alone, which is another reason I wanted to become a mail-order bride and start a family. I can read and write and am very good with numbers...

Mrs. Pettigrew noticed Ebba had stopped. She frowned at her as she filed a fingernail. "Whatever is the matter?"

"I'm not sure what else to say."

"Did you tell him you can cook, sew, clean, read, write…"

"Yes, I told him all of that."

"Tell him you have all of your teeth. That is always a good selling point."

"Selling point?"

"*Oui.* He will know you are healthy at least."

Ebba shrugged.

...and I have all my teeth. I hope you have all of yours. I look forward to hearing from you and what you think about the two of us becoming husband and wife.
Sincerely,
Ebba Knudsen

She put the pen down, turned the paper around and slid it back across the desk.

Mrs. Pettigrew picked it up, gave it a quick read and set it back down. "This will do nicely."

Ebba sighed in relief. "Good. Now what do I do?"

"Now we wait until he sends another letter. If he likes yours, he will likely send train and stage fare as well. Then off you go."

Ebba blinked in astonishment. "Just like that?"

Mrs. Pettigrew snapped her fingers. "Just like that."

"I had no idea it was so easy."

"*Oui*, very easy. Now leave everything to me!" Mrs. Pettigrew said with a wide smile and stood. Ebba got up as the woman came around the desk. She took Ebba's hands in hers and gave them both a squeeze. "You will be very happy as the new Mrs. Weaver!"

"How can you be so sure?"

"Trust me, *ma petite*! I know these things!"

Ebba smiled. "I trust you."

"*Tres bien!* Now off you go!" Mrs. Pettigrew began to usher her to the door.

"When will I hear back from him?"

"It usually takes about a month. Until then, concentrate on making yourself a beautiful bride!"

Ebba couldn't help but smile at the woman's enthusiasm. "What if he doesn't think I'm beautiful?"

Mrs. Pettigrew smiled. "Trust me, *ma cherie*, he will love you from the moment he sees you!"

"You sound so confident. I wish I was."

"Nonsense, you will see! Now run along." Mrs. Pettigrew opened the door of her office.

"Oh no." Ebba took a step toward the door.

"What is this *oh no*?"

"I… I have no wedding dress. What if he says yes and…oh dear…"

"You sew, yes? So you make one."

"Oh, but Mrs. Pettigrew… I'm afraid I can't, not on what I earn. Even if I did have the time, I could never afford the fabric for a proper dress."

"No dress?!" the woman squeaked. "What bride gets married in anything but a wedding dress? This will never do!"

Ebba stared at her wide-eyed as Mrs. Pettigrew began to pace around her office. "But there's nothing I can do," she said weakly.

Mrs. Pettigrew stopped her pacing and pointed at her. "Leave everything to me!"

"But…"

"No buts! You leave, go home and do as I say. Make yourself beautiful!" She shoved Ebba out the door and into the hall. "I will send word as soon as I hear from Mr. Weaver."

"But Mrs. Pettigrew…"

The door slammed shut.

Ebba slumped. "… I don't know how to be beautiful." With a sigh, she turned and trudged down the hall. It was time to go to work. She hoped Mr. Weaver thought raw hands were a thing of beauty, because after a month of her doing laundry for Mrs. Feldnick, that's what he would get.

Mrs. Pettigrew slowly opened the door to her office and peeked into the hall. She caught sight of Ebba as she turned the corner toward the staircase that led to the first floor of the building. With a satisfied smile, she closed the door and hurried to her desk. She picked up the letter Ebba had penned and read it once more.

"Tsk, tsk, tsk. Oh, *ma belle*, this will never light a spark in his eyes. Hmmm…" She set the letter on the desk, snatched up the pen, dipped it in the ink and began to scribble something under Ebba's signature. "There! *That* will get his attention! Ha!" She chuckled to herself then rubbed her hands together in satisfaction. "Now I must see about a wedding dress for the poor girl."

She crossed the office to a coat tree, removed her cloak and hat, donned them and went out the door. It was also time for Adelia Pettigrew to go to work.

Nowhere, Washington Territory,
two weeks later…

Daniel Weaver stood at the counter of the mercantile and tore open the letter his cousin Matthew Quinn had just handed him. His eyes began to water, and he wiped his arm across them to clear his vision. "I'm so nervous, I cain't read it!"

"Give it to me," Matthew said from behind the counter and held out his hand.

Daniel complied. "What's it say? No, wait! Maybe you oughta read it to yerself first, then just tell me if'n she said no."

Matthew rolled his eyes. "If she said no, she'd have done it at the bridal agency."

Daniel glanced at him. "Aw yeah…"

Matthew shoved his spectacles up his nose and perused the letter. *"Dear Mr. Weaver…"*

"I said not out loud!" Daniel whined.

Matthew rolled his eyes again. "For Heaven's sake, Daniel, what are you afraid of? No mail-order bride ever sends a letter of rejection to a man. Unless he's already proposed, which you haven't." He shook the letter in his hand and resumed. "Dear Mr. Weaver…"

"Just get to the good part."

Matthew frowned. "Good part?"

"Yeah."

Matthew rubbed his face with his free hand and looked as if he was counting to ten. He looked at the letter again, then proceeded to read rapidly aloud:

My name is Ebba Knudsen. Mrs. Pettigrew of the Pettigrew Bridal Agency has assured me that you would make a good match. Let me tell you a little about myself and you can be the judge.

I am twenty years old. My parents came to America from Sweden, and our family moved to Denver from Chicago about a year ago because their doctor thought the air here would be good for them. Alas, they are now dead…

Matthew and Daniel exchanged a look of alarm. Matthew swallowed hard and continued:

…Because of this, I have decided to become a mail-order bride. Mrs. Pettigrew comes highly recommended, so I sought her help.

I am five feet and three inches tall with blonde hair and green eyes. I am a hard worker and would keep your house clean and can sew for you.

*I am a fair cook, though my parents thought I was
excellent. I learned to cook from both my mother
and my* mormor *(Swedish for grandmother)...*

"Swedish—that's interesting," Matthew said.

"Is that anythin' like Eye-talian?" Daniel asked.
"You know, like Bella, Calvin's wife?"

"Well...they're both from Europe, but other than
that, no. Completely different." Matthew cleared his
throat and went on:

*...I have no brothers or sisters and no family
left to me in this country. I don't like being alone,
which is another reason I wanted to become a
mail-order bride and start a family. I can read
and write and am very good with numbers and
I have all my teeth...*

He stopped and began to chuckle.

"What's so funny?" Daniel demanded.

Matthew grinned. *"And I hope you have all of
yours,"* he recited slowly.

Daniel smiled brilliantly.

Matthew laughed and returned to the letter. "Ah,
let's see... *I look forward to hearing from you and
what you think about the two of us becoming husband
and wife. Sincerely, Ebba Knudsen. P.S....*" Then his
eyes went wide as his smile faded. He shook his head.
"Good heavens, what the..." He looked at Daniel as
his mouth opened, then back at the letter. "I don't believe it!"

"Believe what? What's it say?" Daniel asked as he leaned over the counter.

Matthew took a few steps back. "What the Sam Hill was this woman thinking?!"

"What?!"

Matthew gaped at him. "I… I…oh my…" He raised an eyebrow and stared at the letter again.

"What's the dang blasted letter say?!" Daniel demanded. He was ready to climb over the counter if Matthew didn't answer.

But just then Betsy Quinn, Matthew's mother and Daniel's aunt, entered from the hall that led to the family's living quarters. Matthew quickly hid the letter behind his back, his face red. "Hello, Mother."

"Why, Daniel! It's so nice to see you!" she said, ignoring her son.

"Howdy, Aunt Betsy. I just came into town to fetch a few supplies and get the mail."

"You'll be spending the night, of course?"

"Sure will. Don't fancy drivin' the wagon home in the dark."

She glanced around the mercantile that she and her husband ran with Matthew and his wife Charlotte. "Did anyone else come with you?"

"No, ma'am, just me."

"Ah, I see," she said with a smile. "Anxious to get your mail, I presume?"

Now it was Daniel's turn to blush. "Ah shucks, Aunt Betsy, ya know I am. Speakin' of which…" He turned to Matthew, who was shaking his head "no" vigorously. "…er… I was kinda hopin' somethin' came for me. Maybe tomorrow." He shot his cousin a warning look, then quickly turned back to his aunt.

"You never know," she said. "Of course, if you do get a letter from a mail-order bride, you know the sheriff will have no problem sending Deputy Turner out to your place to deliver it. That man loves going out there."

"Him and his wife, Rose, both do," Daniel agreed.

His aunt smiled. "You know, sometimes I wonder what would have happened if Charlotte had married Deputy Turner instead of Matthew."

"Perish the thought," Matthew said in protest.

She turned to him. "It could have happened."

"It almost did," Matthew replied accusingly.

Daniel remembered *that* mess. About five years ago, Aunt Betsy had ordered poor Cousin Matty a mail-order bride without telling him. Matty returned home from college, eager to reunite with Charlotte Davis, the local girl he'd grown up with, only to find a mail-order bride on his doorstep the next day. He was furious, but his mother was determined to have her way.

"Well…it all turned out," Aunt Betsy said with a placating smile. "And Matthew, I'm glad you and Charlotte are so happy. Now if you'd just give me some grandchildren, *I'd* be happy too!" With a swish of her skirt, she disappeared back down the hall before either man could comment.

"It's not for lack of trying," Matthew mumbled under his breath. Then he recalled the letter in his hand, and craned his neck to make sure his mother was truly gone before re-reading the postscript. "Wow."

Daniel was still frustrated. "What's that 'wow' supposed to mean?"

Matthew folded the letter, put it back in its envelope and handed it to Daniel. "Just what I said. Wow."

Daniel glanced between his cousin and the letter. "If'n ya say so, Matty." Now he was more curious than ever. "Did she say she was pretty?"

Matthew tried to stifle a chuckle. "Something like that. I think you should write her back right away. She sounds…like an interesting match. Just what you're looking for."

"She does? Well, that's good news!"

"Indeed it is," Matthew agreed, turning to the shelves behind the counter. He grabbed a feather duster and set to work. "Oh, did Aunt Mary give you a list for me to fill?"

"Aw yeah." Daniel searched his pockets. "Hmmm, I know it's here somewhere…"

"Well, when you find it, just set it on the counter."

"Doggone, where'd I put that thing?" Daniel lamented as he patted his shirt pocket. He shrugged and went through them all again. "Oh, here it is!"

Matthew glanced at him over his shoulder. "I'll fill it tomorrow before you leave, how's that?"

"Sounds good to me. I'm kinda hungry. Think I'll go see what Aunt Betsy has on the stove if'n ya don't mind."

"Sure. Supper will be ready soon. Don't eat too much or she'll take a stick to you."

"I won't." Daniel headed for the hallway that led

to the kitchen. "After supper, can ya help me write a letter back?"

Matthew smiled. He'd helped two of his Weaver cousins write their letters to prospective brides; what was one more? Besides, he was willing to do just about anything to get his boisterous cousins to settle down. Then they wouldn't be in his hair so much every time they came to town for supplies.

The bell above the door rang. Matthew turned—and suppressed a wince. "Good afternoon, Mrs. Davis. What can I do for you?"

"I just need a few things, Matthew," his mother in-law, Nellie Davis, replied as she made her way to the counter. "By the way, is my daughter in the back?"

"No, I'm afraid not. Charlotte's out at the Riley farm visiting. But she should be home soon."

"Again? Good grief, does the girl think she lives there?" Mrs. Davis drawled in her sharp Southern accent. She patted her perfectly coiffed hair with a huff.

Matthew shrugged. "You know how close she is with Summer and Elle Riley. Besides, she likes playing with the children."

Mrs. Davis nodded. "Yes, I suppose she does, seeing as how the two of you haven't been able to…"

"Do you have a list for me?" he quickly interjected.

"Certainly—why else would I be here?" She reached into her reticule to pull out her list.

Matthew turned and scrambled up a ladder to fetch something from a high shelf. "Just set it on the counter next to Daniel's. I'll get to it in a minute."

"Oh, all right." She set it down, then glanced at

Daniel's list—and spotted the envelope underneath it. "Has your cousin heard anything from his prospective bride?" she inquired innocently.

"Yes, as a matter of fact he did," Matthew called down as he rifled through a stack of boxes on the shelf.

"Is that so?" she said as she deftly extracted the letter from beneath the list. She suppressed a rush of excitement by biting her lip. "And has he read it?"

"Yes, ma'am, he has."

"What did she say?"

"That's my cousin's business. You'll have to ask him."

"Of course." She quickly slid the letter out of its envelope.

"Why, Nellie!" Betsy Quinn called from the hall. "How are you?"

Nellie did what any self-respecting gossip would do—she stuffed the letter into her reticule. "Betsy! How nice to see you. I need a few things, if you don't mind. Matthew would see to my list but he seems to be preoccupied at the moment."

Betsy glanced at her son atop his perch. "What are you doing up there?"

"I'm getting something down before I forget. Deputy Turner told me yesterday he'd try to get in here before closing for a new pair of boots. Where did we put the new black ones?"

"On the opposite side. I swear I told you that yesterday."

"No, Mother, I'm afraid you didn't," Matthew

groaned and began to climb down the ladder. "You probably just thought you did."

"He has a point, Betsy. The older we get, the more forgetful we become," Mrs. Davis replied. "Now about my list?"

"Yes, let me take care of it." She went behind the counter, picked up the list and quickly read it. She then noticed the other one. "Matthew, is this Daniel's?"

"Yes, Mother. I told him I would fill it early in the morning before he left. No sense doing it now."

"Now or later makes no difference to me—just don't lose it." She handed it to him as he reached the floor. "You're going to help him with his return letter, aren't you?" Before he could answer she turned to Mrs. Davis. "Daniel just told me he finally heard back from his mail-order bride! Isn't that wonderful?"

"Wonderful," Mrs. Davis agreed as she gripped her reticule tighter. "I can't wait to hear more."

"I'd love to tell you, but I don't have time. Let me get you what you need, then I've got to get a batch of biscuits in the oven."

"That's quite all right," said Mrs. Davis. "I'm sure to hear all about it tomorrow."

"Oh, of course you will!" Betsy agreed. "Trust me, you'll be the first!"

Mrs. Davis smiled. "Yes, I know."

Chapter Three

Later that evening, Daniel leaned over the kitchen table as Matthew penned his letter for him.

Dear Miss Knudsen:
I've received your letter and I think you would make me a fine wife...

"Wait a minute, Matty," Daniel said. "Don't ya need to re-read the letter she sent? What if ya leave somethin' important out?"

Matthew snorted. "I know all there is to know about Miss Knudsen and her wifely...capabilities. She made it quite clear in her letter. Trust me, I don't need to see it again to do this."

"All right, if'n ya say so. I was just figgerin'."

Matthew nodded tersely. "Now where was I? Ah yes..."

...and look forward to the day when we can finally meet. I have enclosed train and stage fare

*for your journey, plus enough funds to cover your
expenses along the way. Send word of your date
of arrival and I will be waiting.*

"There, that should do it," Matthew said. He shoved
the paper and pen at Daniel. "Here, you can sign it
now."

"But my handwritin' ain't as nice as yers, cousin."

"Just sign it. It wouldn't be right if I did…oh, wait!"
Matthew grabbed the pen back again.

"Hey! What're ya doin'?"

Matthew grinned at him, scribbled something down,
then handed the pen back. "There, now it's done."

Daniel looked at it:

*P.S. And just to let you know, I have all my teeth
too…among other things.*

Daniel's face scrunched up in confusion. "What
other things?"

"Never mind, just sign it," he ordered.

"Fine. But next time I need a letter writ, I'm gonna
do it myself." Daniel scrawled his signature across the
bottom of the page. "Here—you'll put this in the post
tomorrow like ya said, right?"

"Of course. I know you're anxious to get your bride
out here. From the sounds of it, she's anxious as well."
He licked his lips to hide a smirk, failed and turned
away instead. "I think I'll go see what Mother's made
for dessert."

"I hope its pie," Daniel commented as Matthew left

the room. From the sound of it, though, he went out the back door. Daniel could hear laughter coming from the stoop, and wondered what had gotten into his cousin. "Maybe married life has him on edge like Ma says."

"Are you talking to yourself, Daniel?" his uncle asked as he entered the room.

"Yessir, I am."

He smiled. "And what does yourself tell you these days?"

"That my cousin out there is a little off."

Mr. Quinn raised a single eyebrow at the statement and turned toward the back door. The cackles on the other side got louder. "I see. Maybe I ought to investigate."

"Don't pay Matty no mind, Uncle. He's got a lot to worry about is all, considerin' he and Charlotte got themselves that little, ya know…problem?"

"Problem?"

Daniel nodded, folded his arms into a cradle and rocked them back and forth.

"Oh yes, that. It happens sometimes, son. I remember it took a few years for you to come along. You're what, five years younger than Calvin and Benjamin?"

"Yessir. Almost to the day."

"I'm sure they're just getting a late start. Nothing wrong with that now, is there?"

"Nossir, I don't think so. But Aunt Betsy don't seem like she agrees."

"Ah yes, your dear Aunt Betsy," Mr. Quinn said with a sigh. "She'll just have to be patient."

"Well if'n Matty and Charlotte don't get the job

done soon, I think Aunt Betsy's patience is gonna run out."

His uncle chuckled. "Well, son, you let me worry about her." He pulled out a chair and sat. "What about you? Do you want children right away?"

"Me?" Daniel asked in shock. "Nossir, not me. We got enough of 'em around the place without me addin' any of my own."

He chuckled again. "You have a good point there. I don't know how your brother Calvin manages. How are they doing, by the way?"

"Calvin and Bella? They're just fine. Everyone is… all twenty-four of us."

"And your mail-order bride will make it twenty-five. You're going to need your own post office out there."

Daniel laughed. "Nah, Ma likes comin' into Nowhere too much. In fact, she'll be with me next time I come to town."

"When will that be?"

"Whenever Matty thinks I'll get another letter from my bride. When I do, she'll be tellin' me what day and time she's gonna get here."

"And soon you'll be a married man," his uncle said with pride. "I have to say, I never thought I'd see the four of you boys wed. Your pa would be mighty proud…mighty proud indeed to see how well you've done for yourselves."

Daniel felt his throat tighten. He was fourteen when his father died and had taken his death the hardest. Not a day went by that he didn't think about him. "I'm sure he would."

"How about some coffee?" his uncle asked as he got up from the table.

Daniel nodded, glad to be off the subject of his pa. It had been nearly ten years since his passing, but some days it seemed like it was only last week. Today was one of those days for some reason and he didn't want to talk about it anymore. "Did Aunt Betsy make a pie?"

"Yep, which means it's hidden somewhere right in this very room," his uncle said with a waggle of his eyebrows. "What say we find it?"

"Sounds good to me."

Mr. Quinn grinned, then went to a hutch. He took out two cups and saucers, set them on the table, then poured them each a cup of coffee. Rubbing his hands together in anticipation, he glanced around the kitchen. "Now where could it be?"

Before either of them made a move, Matthew waltzed into the room, a pie in his hand. "Found it!"

His father stared at him in amazement. "I didn't even get a chance to look!"

Daniel laughed. "Where was it?"

"Storeroom, top left shelf."

Mr. Quinn burst into hysterics. "The top shelf?"

"The *very* top shelf," Matthew said. "She's making it harder and harder for us, Pa."

"That she is," his father agreed. "C'mon, boys, let's have some, then put it back!"

"Won't Aunt Betsy get mad?" Daniel asked.

"Sure!" said his uncle. "That's half the fun!"

Daniel scratched his head. "I got me a lot to learn about bein' married."

"Don't worry. You've got at least a month to figure out a few things before your bride gets here," his uncle assured.

"What kind of things?" Daniel asked.

Matthew almost choked as he stole a sip of his father's coffee. He laughed half-heartedly. "Don't worry. A lot of what you need to learn will just come…naturally."

Daniel and his uncle exchanged a look of confusion.

"Never mind," Matthew said. "Let's have some pie."

Nowhere, Washington Territory,
June 1876

"I can hardly believe it's been four years since I've been here. The last time there was also a wedding for a mail-order bride, only she wasn't Swedish—she was Eye-talian. Pretty as a picture, too. Wait a minute, did I already tell you about her?"

"No, Sheriff Hughes," Ebba said. "You told me about your sister Leona and her family." Not to mention his town of Clear Creek, the brothers Cooke and their huge ranch and all sorts of tall tales, half of which she didn't believe. Heavens, but the man was a talker!

Harlan Hughes sighed and tapped his head with a finger. "My memory ain't what it used to be, I'm afraid. That's one of the reasons I'm here, aside from visiting my sister and nephews. There's a deputy working here, Tom Turner, that I'm going to try to talk into coming back to Clear Creek."

"You need another deputy?" she asked.

"No. I want Tom to take over as sheriff."

She looked the man up and down. He didn't look that old, maybe his late fifties, but what did she know? Maybe he was just tired of the job. "You wish to retire?"

"Among other things," he said. "But enough about me. You're going to love Nowhere. I know it's kind of a funny name for a town, but it'll grow on you."

"Do you visit your sister a lot?"

"I used to, but I've just been too busy lately. I can't wait to see my grandnephews and grandnieces. Spencer, my sister's son, he's the sheriff in town. His older brother Clayton was the sheriff before him, but he went back to apple farming."

Ebba suddenly sneezed. It was as if the word "farming" set her affliction off.

"Oh, that's too bad," the sheriff said. "And you were doing so well too. I think it's been at least three hours since you sneezed last."

Ebba pulled a handkerchief out of her reticule and blew her nose, her eyes filling with tears. Hopefully the sheriff wouldn't notice they were tears of frustration. She'd sneezed and hacked her way across the country—the trains weren't too bad, but ever since she'd switched to traveling by stagecoach she'd had a time of it. She blew her nose again. "I don't know how I'm going to survive this place, Sheriff Hughes."

He reached over and patted her on the shoulder. "There, now, Miss Knudsen. I'm sure the doc in town can help you. I know our doc from Clear Creek could— Doc Drake can fix whatever ails anyone. And Doc

Brown in Nowhere is a fine man too. He and his wife Millie will come up with something."

"I know I'm not the only one that suffers so, but from what I've been told, there is no cure other than a different climate."

"What sort of climate?"

"I hear that living near the sea is supposed to be good."

Sheriff Hughes shook his head. "I'm afraid there's no sea around here, Miss Knudsen. But don't worry, I'll check around town and see if anyone has some sort of remedy. You can't be the only one to suffer sneezing fits."

"I'm sure I'm not." She swallowed hard and dabbed at her watering eyes, blinking a few times to clear them. She wanted to observe the beautiful countryside, as the road cut through a gently rolling landscape full of apple, pear and cherry orchards. In the distance were the legendary forests and mountains of the Northwest. It was lovely…to look at. But the air made her sneeze and hack until she couldn't see straight. How was she ever to live in this place?

Suddenly a line of wooden buildings came into view. "Nowhere! Now entering Nowhere!" the driver called from his perch atop the stagecoach.

Sheriff Hughes peered out the window, a huge smile on his face. "Well, Miss Knudsen, here we are! Trust me when I tell you, you're going to love it! Like I said before, Nowhere is a wonderful little town." He suddenly straightened. "Great Scott, I forgot to ask—who is your intended?"

"Daniel Weaver is his name."

Sheriff Hughes looked at her in shock. "Daniel *Weaver*?"

Ebba's heart leapt into her throat. *Oh no, is there something wrong with the man?* Sheriff Hughes must know him; he'd been here often enough from the sound of it. "You...have met him?"

"Well, of course—I know the whole Weaver clan! Wonderful people! I plan on spending a lot of time out there this trip."

"You do?" she said in surprise. *Well, that's a relief,* she thought. "What is he like, my intended?"

"Young Daniel is the only one of those boys not yet hitched. It's about time he got himself a wife. You're marrying into a fine family, Miss Knudsen."

Ebba closed her eyes with a sigh. "That is good to know, Sheriff."

The stagecoach slowed as they reached the center of town and Ebba had a sudden burst of excitement. "This is it!"

"Yes, it certainly is," the sheriff agreed, a happy gleam in his eye.

Ebba caught the look and smiled. "You must be very excited to see your sister and nephews."

"And a few other folks. Looks like you and I will be seeing each other a lot while I'm here."

"Yes, I'm sure we will." She took her handkerchief and dabbed at her nose. "I must look a mess."

"You look fine. Daniel's ma is good at mixing things up to fix an ailment. It's like I said before, the folks in this town will do what they can to help you."

"I have never lived in a small town before. You make it sound so nice."

"Because it is, Miss Knudsen," he said as the stage came to a stop.

"Nowhere, folks!" the stagecoach driver called.

Ebba's heart fluttered. She was about to meet her intended! She hoped her nose wasn't as red as it felt. How could it not be, as often as she blew it? But Daniel Weaver would have to get used to that. So would everyone else in town, for that matter.

The driver climbed down and opened the stagecoach door. "Let me help you, miss," he said, then got a good look at her. "Er...are you okay?"

"Yes. It's just all the sneezing, you see."

"Yeah," he said as he stared. "I *do* see."

Her eyes widened and she quickly glanced around. Lovely. Her nose was probably as red as a cherry! "I think it's from all the trees here. The orchards..."

The stagecoach driver gulped. "I hope you're here for a short visit then, missy, or you're in for a heap of suffering."

Tears stung the back of her eyes. "I'm here to get married," she said weakly.

"Oh. I'm sorry." He made it sound as if someone had just died. At the moment, she felt like she certainly could. She didn't want her intended to see her like this, but what could she do? She took the hand the driver offered and disembarked.

Sheriff Hughes followed and stood next to her, glancing around. "I don't see Leona anywhere."

"Do you see my intended?"

"No, none of the Weaver clan. I wonder where everyone is."

A woman stared down at them from the boardwalk in front of a mercantile. She was well dressed and stood like she owned the place. *Maybe she's the mayor's wife,* Ebba mused. That is, if the town was big enough to have a mayor. "Who is that?" she asked.

Sheriff Hughes turned, spied the woman and said in a low voice, "That's Nellie Davis. She'll probably know where folks are. She makes it a point to know *everything* that goes on in this town."

The driver snorted in response, pulling Ebba's attention from the woman. She looked at him as he quickly composed himself. "I'll just…get your bags." He scrambled up to the top of the stagecoach.

Ebba looked again at the woman, who looked down her nose at her in disdain. Now why would that be?

"Mrs. Davis!" the sheriff called. "Have you seen Leona or any of the Weavers around?"

"Last time I saw any of them, they were down at Hank's restaurant having coffee," she said loftily.

Ebba suddenly felt self-conscious. She dabbed at her nose with the handkerchief. Why was her intended drinking coffee when he knew she was arriving?

The sheriff pulled out a pocket watch and flipped it open. "Well, I'll be—we're fifteen minutes early! How about that?" He turned to Ebba. "What say we go down to Hank's and surprise them?"

Ebba smiled at the suggestion for three reasons. She'd be meeting her intended. Her scratchy throat could desperately use a hot drink. And it would get her away from the piercing gaze of this Nellie Davis person. "Yes, that's a good idea, Sheriff."

As soon as their bags hit the ground, he picked them up and nodded toward the end of the street. "Hank's is this way—follow me."

"Welcome to Nowhere," Mrs. Davis called condescendingly.

Ebba looked at her and wondered what could have happened to the woman to make her so hostile to a stranger. "Thank you," she said as politely as she could.

Mrs. Davis looked her up and down, then spun on her heel and marched into the mercantile.

Sheriff Hughes watched the door slam shut. "I wonder what's in her craw today?" He shook his head. "Something always is. You'll want to watch out for her. All in all, Nellie Davis is harmless, but she can get uppity. Her daughter Charlotte used to be just like her, but she's changed into a right fine woman. She works in the mercantile with her husband Matthew— who happens to be the cousin of the man you're going to marry."

Ebba smiled. "You know everyone in this town, don't you, Sheriff Hughes?"

He thought a moment. "Pretty much. Now let's go find your intended, shall we?"

She smiled again. "Yes, let's."

The sheriff led Ebba up the street. She took note of the buildings and the townspeople as they went about their daily business. Several waved at Sheriff Hughes, who waved or called out a greeting in return. It was quite apparent that everyone knew him.

But no one asked who she was. Instead they stared in curiosity or (at least from the women) looked at her similarly to Mrs. Davis. Did the people here not like strangers? They certainly weren't making her feel very welcome.

"Here we are!" the sheriff announced as they reached Hank's Restaurant. He stuck one bag under his arm so he could open the door, then motioned for her to precede him. With her heart in her throat, she stepped inside.

Chapter Four

No one noticed the sheriff and Ebba as they entered the restaurant. Ebba took the opportunity to search for her intended. But which one was he? There were quite a few men seated at the various tables. And every table looked full—not surprising, as it was lunchtime.

"Land sakes, what are you doing here?" a woman exclaimed as she stood. She was older, probably around the same age as the sheriff and with a similar face. His sister, perhaps?

"Leona!" he said with a smile and quickly crossed the room to her, dropping the bags as he gave her a hug. Two men seated at the table stood, went to the sheriff and gave him the same sort of greeting.

Ebba stood quietly to one side and watched, then noticed that others weren't watching the sheriff and his sister, but her. Some of the men looked her up and down like she was a piece of candy, while the women stared in disdain before turning away. All except a petite middle-aged woman with an enormous hat on her head—she stood slowly, then smacked the shoulder of a young man who was busy watching the sheriff, his back to Ebba. The man slowly turned in his chair…

Ebba's breath caught. *Åh herregud,* she thought to herself. Oh my—he was *gorgeous*! She swallowed hard and willed herself not to sweat, as the room suddenly felt much warmer.

He stood, looked at her, then slowly smiled. But before he could say anything, the woman headed straight for her. "My my, aren't you a vision!" She turned to the young man, who was also approaching. "Isn't she? Didn't I tell you she'd be beautiful?"

He stopped, eyes wide, and swallowed hard. "Yeah, Ma, ya did." His eyes widened even further as he smacked his forehead with the palm of his hand. "Oh! I'm so sorry! We plumb meant to meet ya when the stage pulled in!"

"It was early," Ebba said softly. Or was she losing her voice, beginning to faint? She'd better get some coffee—quickly.

"It was?" the woman said in surprise. "Of all the days for it to be early. Doesn't that just figure? We're sorry, child. It's like Daniel said—we really did mean to meet you at the stage."

Ebba smiled, afraid to use her voice. The woman was rambling but she didn't care. She glanced at Sheriff Hughes, who pointed at the man standing in front of her and mouthed *Daniel Weaver.*

She nodded in acknowledgment, then turned back to her intended. He just stood and stared at her, and she wondered if she'd come as a shock. She then remembered her poor nose and fought a shudder of embarrassment. She hoped he wasn't disappointed in how she looked. "Would it be too much trouble," she rasped, "to get a cup of coffee?"

"Of course not, dear," the woman said. "Oh, where are my manners? I'm Mary Weaver. I'm going to be your new mother-in-law!"

Ebba smiled. "Pleased to meet you," she croaked. Great, her voice was giving out completely!

"Oh, you poor child," Mrs. Weaver said. "Do you have a cold?"

It was all Ebba could do not to groan. "Something like that."

"Daniel, pull out a chair for the lady," she ordered, then pointed at the table. "Hank! Some coffee!" she yelled.

A middle-aged man stomped out from the kitchen. "Good grief, you don't have to shout like that. If you wanted some that badly, you know where the pot is!"

"This isn't my restaurant, it's yours," she shot back. "Now pour a cup for this poor child—she's had a long journey."

Hank studied Ebba a moment. "So this is Daniel's mail-order bride. Now ain't he a lucky son of a gun?"

"He's right there, Hank, and so is she," Mrs. Weaver scolded. "Now stop looking at her like that and give her some coffee!"

He quickly complied. For such a small thing, the woman had a tremendous air of authority about her. Ebba was glad she did, as she wasn't sure about the look the restaurant owner had been giving her. Apparently the townspeople here had a low opinion of strangers.

"Would you like to sit down?" her intended asked as he pulled out a chair.

"Yes," she said, or at least tried to; her voice was almost gone. She hated when this happened. She hoped this wasn't going to be the norm the entire time she lived here. *If* she could live here. What was she going to do when her affliction became too much for her?

She practically fell into the chair. Good grief—should she even marry this man? Would she be able to do the things required of a farmer's wife if she was constantly sneezing and coughing? What if he didn't want to put up with it? That was something she hadn't considered until now.

She nodded in thanks as Hank placed a cup of coffee in front of her, reached for it and took a sip. The hot brew hit her raw throat and she cringed in pain.

"Is everything all right?" Mr. Weaver asked. "Is the coffee too hot?"

"A little," she said. But her voice sounded better already.

"Land sakes, child," Mrs. Weaver said. "Have you not been well?"

Sheriff Hughes was suddenly at her side. "The poor thing coughed and sneezed nearly half the trip."

"Is that so?" Mrs. Weaver said. "I know just what you need, but I'm afraid I'll have to go to the saloon."

"The saloon?" Ebba asked in shock. "What do you need from there?"

"Isn't it obvious?" asked the sheriff with a chuckle.

"But don't worry none—Mary here can fix you right up."

"You stay right there, dear, and I'll hurry back as fast as I can," Mrs. Weaver said with a smile.

"I'll go with you," the sheriff offered. "A woman ought not to be barging into the saloon by herself. Especially when it's you—you're liable to scare the men half to death."

Mary Weaver laughed. "Oh Harlan, don't be silly."

"Yeah," agreed Daniel. "She's liable to scare 'em *completely* to death!"

Ebba couldn't help but grin, even though she wasn't quite sure what they were talking about. "Do you really think you can make something that will help? This has been a problem of mine for a long time."

"Common occurrence around here," Mrs. Weaver said. "You aren't the first to cough and sneeze around these parts, and you won't be the last, trust me."

Ebba's heart swelled. She wasn't the only one? Of course she knew that, but she'd never been around people that had things as bad as she did. "Then by all means, don't let me keep you, Mrs. Weaver."

"Daniel, why don't you order up this pretty thing some lunch?" his mother suggested. "The two of you can get acquainted while Harlan and I take care of business."

"Sure, Ma. I'll take good care of her." He met Ebba's gaze and smiled shyly.

She studied him and had to agree with his first letter. He had beautiful eyes, and for a second she saw a part of his heart staring back. But could that be?

They'd only just met. "Does this place have a menu?" she asked him, unable to think of anything else to say.

"Kind of—depends on what day it is. This bein' Tuesday, it's beef stew."

"As long as it's hot, that's what matters."

"Are ya cold?"

"No, it's just that my throat feels so raw from coughing." Maybe she shouldn't have told him that, but it's not like she hadn't said so already. And if they were going to marry, better he know now.

"You'll like Hank's beef stew. It's not as good as Ma's or Samijo's, but it'll do in a pinch."

"Who is Samijo?"

"She's my sister-in-law. She's married to my brother Arlan. They were gonna come with us to pick ya up, but one of their younguns got hisself a bellyache day before yesterday."

"Is he still not feeling well?"

"Don't rightly know. I ain't seen him since early yesterday mornin'."

It took Ebba a moment to absorb that. "You mean you've been in town since yesterday?"

"Sure have."

She blinked a few times, unsure of what to say next. Why would they have come to town yesterday when the stage didn't come until now? Maybe they had a lot of business to attend to and decided to spend the night? "Well," she said. "I hope he feels better soon."

"Oh, he will—he always does. But he's got what ya might call a sensitive stomach. That's what Doc Brown calls it anyway."

Ebba smiled. "How many children does your brother have?" she asked as Hank approached their table again.

"Three—two boys and a girl." He turned to Hank. "Could you bring this pretty lady a bowl of your beef stew, please?" Hank grunted some sort of response before he turned and headed for the kitchen. "Don't mind Hank," Mr. Weaver said. "He gets grumpy like that 'bout this time of day. Probably 'cause of all the dishes he's gonna hafta wash."

Ebba glanced around. "Doesn't he have any help?"

"Not right now. Folks 'round here can either make more money workin' the orchards, or they're too young. Not much in between as far as workers at the moment."

She glanced around the room again and noticed more than one person staring back. She quickly looked down into her coffee cup, picked it up and took a sip. It felt good and took her mind off the curious stares.

"I'm sure glad yer here," he said.

She raised her eyes to his and swore she got another tiny glimpse into his heart. This was a good man, she could tell. "So am I. It was a long journey."

"Ma got ya a room at the hotel. She and I are stayin' with my Aunt Betsy at the mercantile. Her family owns it."

There was something strange about what he'd just said. Hadn't Sheriff Hughes mentioned something about the mercantile? "I thought your cousin did."

"Harlan must've told ya that. Yeah, Matty will one day, but right now his ma and pa do, and he and his wife Charlotte work there."

"Oh yes, the sheriff did tell me that."

"Yeah, good old Harlan. Sure is good to see him— been a long time since he's come to Nowhere."

"He mentioned coming to your farm. He plans to visit you and your family a lot while he's here."

Daniel winked conspiratorially. "Sure he does, on account he's kinda sweet on Ma."

"He is?" she said with a smile. "Does she feel the same way about him?"

"Far as we can tell."

"Did you know he was coming?"

"Oh yeah. Clayton, Harlan's nephew, told us about a month ago, and Ma's been fussin' around the house ever since. She even wore her new favorite hat today."

Ebba giggled. "I think that's wonderful. It will be fun to watch them."

"Yeah, speakin' of that…" He leaned toward her. "I noticed quite a few folks are watchin' ya kinda funny-like. I don't understand why—they all knew I had a mail-order bride comin'. Heck, a lot of them have known for months."

She shrugged. She didn't have an answer. "Are folks here normally like this?"

"What do ya mean?"

How was she going to put this? "Well…some of them don't seem very friendly."

"People in Nowhere not friendly? That don't make no sense. Folks around here are some of the friendliest you'll ever find. Everyone that comes here says so." He glanced around the room again. "Now that ya mention it, I do notice a few looks that ain't…well, normal."

"That's what I mean. They seem to be looking at me rather oddly."

He studied her a moment. "Hey," he said. "Ya got an accent! I just noticed!"

"So do you," she pointed out.

"I do?" he asked in surprise.

"Yes."

He cocked his head to one side. "An accent? Well, how 'bout that? I never knew I had one. Folks 'round here all sorta sound alike."

She laughed at that, then began to cough. He reached over and gently patted her back. "Thank you," she said and then took another sip of coffee, hoping it would suppress her hacking. It wasn't as hot as before, but did do the job.

"Ya poor thing, did ya really do that half the trip like Harlan said?"

She nodded. "And then some."

"Well, don't ya worry none—Ma is really good at whippin' up remedies. And if she cain't, Doc Brown can."

Hank brought her stew and set it on the table. "You want any?" he asked her intended.

"No, Hank, I'm fine. I'll just sit here and watch my future bride enjoy hers."

Ebba blushed. She hadn't thought about eating in front of him, let alone him watching her do it. Good heavens, what if she spilled something on herself? Having a coughing fit in front of him was bad enough.

"Ya go ahead and eat that there stew, sweetie," he said. "Ya look like ya need it."

Ebba half-smiled. He had no idea.

* * *

She was lovely. Not beautiful like his sister-in-law Isabella, who looked as if she'd been carved out of the finest marble and should be put on display. No, his mail-order bride was a different kind of beautiful, one he couldn't quite put into words.

Daniel watched her take her first bite of stew. She hesitated, blew on a spoonful to cool it, then delicately put it into her mouth. The sight made his head spin. He wasn't sure he'd make it through the meal.

"It's good," she said.

"Hank does all right. His roast beef is tough sometimes…"

"I heard that," Hank said as he hurried past their table, his arms laden with dirty dishes.

"Ya need some help there, Hank?" Daniel asked.

Hank stopped. "Are you offering, Danny boy?"

"We ain't leavin' 'til tomorrow. And ya do look like ya got yer hands full, kinda literal-like."

Hank laughed. "If your bride don't mind, then I sure don't."

"Ya don't mind, do ya, sweetie?"

She looked between him and Hank as he headed for the kitchen. "Maybe I can help."

"Ya eat first," he told her. "It looks like it's helpin' ya."

"What do you mean, looks like?"

"Before, ya were kinda pale. I guess Hank's stew put some color back in yer cheeks. Sit a minute and finish yer lunch. I'm just gonna help him out. Unless ya need me to stay?"

"It's all right—you go ahead."

"Thanks, sweetie. This won't take long." He smiled, got up and followed Hank into the kitchen. Once there, he stopped for a deep breath.

"That little lady make you nervous, son?" Hank asked.

"I wasn't expectin' her to be so pretty. I didn't think I'd get as lucky as my brothers, 'specially Calvin. Look who he got!"

"A woman can be the most beautiful thing in the world, but if she's a harpy, what good is all that beauty?" Hank asked as he dumped dishes into a metal tub. "I'll wash, you dry."

"Fair 'nough. Ya ever been married, Hank?"

"A long time ago, before I ever came out West. Lily was her name. Prettiest thing on two legs."

"What happened to her?"

"Influenza. I'd never seen anyone cough up so much blood in my life. Terrible business. That's something I never want to see again."

"I'm sorry, Hank. I never knew ya had a wife, and here I've lived here all my life."

"It's not something I talk about. What for? Unless someone comes along and asks."

Daniel took up a dishrag and waited for Hank to hand him something to dry. "Does anyone else know ya were married before?"

"Mr. Davis does. I told him one day when he was the only one in here, having some coffee and pie."

"Ya told Mr. Davis and the whole town still don't know?!" Daniel asked in shock.

"That's because he obviously never told *Mrs.* Davis," Hank commented, handing him a plate.

They spent the next several minutes washing and drying before a knock sounded at the doorway. Daniel turned to see Ebba with her bowl in her hand. "I'm afraid I'm going to have to add one more to your pile, gentlemen."

Daniel smiled. "The more the merrier, I hear tell. Bring it on in and we'll take care of it."

No sooner had she stepped forward than a man took her place. "Hey, Hank, can I get some coffee and pie?"

"Sure," Hank said. "Here, Daniel, you take over." He wiped his hands on his apron and headed into the dining area, coffee pot in hand.

Daniel watched him go, then turned to Ebba. "I'll take over the washin' if'n you'll take over the dryin'."

She smiled tentatively. "All right."

Daniel plunged his hands into the metal tub and flinched. "Hank must've just poured a kettle of hot water into this—it's warmer than I expected." He scrubbed a plate, dipped it into a smaller tub of water to rinse it, then handed it to her. "I bet the last thing ya expected when ya got off the stage was doin' dishes."

"You're quite right," she said with a small giggle. "Maybe he won't charge me for the stew."

"That's somethin' ya wouldn't have to worry about anyway. I'm payin' for yer lunch."

"I thought that might be the case, but on the other hand, if you don't have to…"

He laughed. "I see what yer saying. Maybe if'n we do these dishes, he won't charge me for nothin'."

"One never knows," she said, her eyes bright. The food had definitely done her some good. Before she'd looked tired, haggard even. But now she seemed right as rain as far as he could tell. Of course, he didn't really know her yet, but that would be remedied the moment they married—in more ways than one.

Until then, Daniel was content to enjoy doing dishes with his future bride.

Chapter Five

Ebba did her best not to stare at her intended. Daniel Weaver was much bigger than she'd first thought, now that she found herself next to him. The top of her head barely reached his shoulder.

But more important than his physique was his character. She had a list of moral attributes she wanted in a husband and hoped he could fill it. Yes, a literal list. She'd worked it up on the train trip west to fill time, revised it here and there along the way, and was now ready to start ticking off Mr. Weaver's qualifications. She at least wanted to know if she'd get most of what she'd hoped for in a husband.

So far she liked that he'd offered to help Hank with the extra workload. That poor man was trying to do everything. Maybe if her husband's farm wasn't too far out of town, she could come help him out a few days a week—perhaps even earn a little extra cash for the family. She wasn't averse to hard work. Besides, being indoors was better than being outdoors, where the air could send her into a fit of sneezing.

"I'm sorry I ain't asked ya yet," Daniel said, "but how was yer journey?"

"Very tiring, but I managed to get some sleep at the last couple of stage stops."

"Did ya stop at the Gundersons'?" he asked. "It's the last stage stop before ya reach Nowhere. We sell fruit to Mrs. Gunderson every year."

"Yes, we did. That's where I met Sheriff Hughes."

"Harlan's a right fine fella. But I already told ya that."

"He certainly is. I...hope he and your mother are able to spend time together, like he plans."

"Bein' as how he was so quick to offer his assistance earlier, it's a good bet they will."

"She was going into a saloon—of course he would offer."

"Yes, but around here everyone knows Ma." He winked. "And I'll let ya in on a little secret."

"What's that?"

"Ma don't need no escort. Once she starts givin' orders, the menfolk 'round here jump to get things done."

"Really? Why is that?"

He shrugged. "Always been like that, for as long as I can remember. She may be little, but she's got more bark to go with her bite than most armies."

Ebba laughed. "I'll be sure to behave myself around her. I wouldn't want to get on her bad side."

"Not much chance of that 'less ya do somethin' real stupid. Trust me, I know."

"Oh dear. I can't imagine what you could have done to bring about her wrath."

To her surprise, he cringed. "Just don't mention wells 'round Ma and you'll be fine."

"Wells?" she asked. "I don't understand."

He chuckled. "Ya will if'n ya mention 'em, especially if'n my name is in the same sentence. Try it one day and see what happens."

She smiled lopsidedly. "I'm not sure I should, not after listening to you."

He was about to reply when his mother walked into the kitchen. "There you are!" Mrs. Weaver crossed the room to where she stood, a glass in her hand. "Here you go, child. Swig this down and you should be fine."

Ebba dried her hands on her dishtowel and stared at the glass. "What is it?"

Mrs. Weaver swirled the brownish liquid around a few times. "My own invention. But I'd better not tell you what's in it 'til *after* you drink it down."

Ebba took an unconscious step backwards and gave the glass a worried look. "Maybe you shouldn't have told me that."

"There's nothing bad about it, child. It might taste a little funny, but trust me, it works."

Ebba steeled herself and reached for the glass. Once she had it in her hand she sniffed at the contents, grimaced and coughed. It had an odd smell that she could not identify—not terrible, but not exactly pleasant either.

"Maybe ya oughta hold your nose when ya down it," Daniel suggested.

"There's an idea," Ebba agreed. "Are you sure this will work? I've seen more than my share of doctors, Mrs. Weaver, and none of their tonics have done much for me."

"This ain't some tonic made by a quack. This here is good wholesome…ingredients."

"Best just drink it, sweetie," Daniel said.

Ebba brought the glass to her lips and took a tentative sip. It didn't taste any better than it looked, but it was drinkable. She looked at Mrs. Weaver. "There are herbs in here. I can taste them."

"Yep—several, in fact. Now drink up. Won't do you any good while it's still in the glass."

Ebba exhaled, took a deep breath and downed the contents in one shot. She coughed and sputtered a few times, almost dropping the glass in the process. "Thank…you…"

Daniel patted her on the back. "Maybe she should drink some water now, Ma."

"No, that stuff needs to coat her throat—it'll help with the coughing. You don't want her hacking all night, do you? Poor thing looks as if she hasn't had a full night's sleep for a week as it is."

"Thank you, Mrs. Weaver," Ebba managed. "I hope it helps."

"It will, you'll see. Now let's get you to the hotel and settled. Then you can rest a while before supper."

"The hotel?" Ebba said. "I don't understand why we're spending the night in town."

"It's on account of everyone who can't attend the weddin'," Daniel said. "Not everyone can make it all the way out to our place, so this way they get a chance to meet ya before we leave."

"Oh." Ebba looked between Daniel and his mother. "We're to be married at your farm?"

"Yep! It'll be a lot nicer than having it in some stuffy old church..." Daniel stopped, then quickly corrected himself. "I mean, not that the church here ain't nice or nothin', but the weather's been right fine lately and I thought it might be nicer to get hitched in one of the orchards."

Ebba smiled as she pictured the two of them standing beneath blossoming apple trees. "I think I'd like that." *Provided I can breathe through it,* she mentally added.

The man actually blushed! "I was kinda hopin' ya would."

A tingle ran up her spine at the boyish look on his face. "Do you have a lot of apple trees?"

"An orchard usually does," he said with a laugh.

Now it was her turn to blush. "I suppose what I meant was, do you have a lot of orchards?"

"Sure do," he said as he studied her face.

"Ahem," Mrs. Weaver said. "The hotel?"

"Oh! Sure, Ma." Daniel offered Ebba his arm.

A sudden shyness came over her and she hesitated to take it. When she finally did, a rush of heat hit as if pulsing through his arm to hers, then through the rest of her body. She'd never felt anything like it and wondered if there was something wrong with her. Maybe his mother's concoction had a few side effects. She blinked a few times to make sure she could still see straight.

"Is somethin' wrong, sweetie?" Daniel asked. "Ya ain't gettin' sick or nothin', are ya?"

"No, not at all. I just felt a little…funny for a moment."

"Best get her to the hotel, son," his mother suggested. "She's going to need to lie down."

Daniel looked from Ebba to his mother and back again. "That right, sweetie? Do ya need to lie down quick-like? If so I can carry ya to the hotel…"

"No!" Ebba blurted. "That won't be necessary!" A sudden picture of him carrying her down the middle of the street made her shudder. It was bad enough she'd gotten all those funny looks from the townspeople. She could just imagine what they'd think of her if they saw that.

"Suit yourself," he said. "But I'll do it if I hafta."

"You won't have to," she said quickly. "I'm sure I'll be fine after I rest for an hour or two."

"Ya sure?" he teased.

"I'm sure," she said with a bemused look.

"Stop antagonizing the poor girl and let's get going!" his mother barked.

Ebba watched him press his lips together as he tried not to laugh. "Right away, Ma."

They left Hank's and went up the street to a small hotel. All in all, the town was very charming—when she wasn't being glared at—and Ebba found herself looking forward to spending more time exploring it after she and Daniel were wed.

Once inside the hotel, they didn't bother going to the desk but headed straight for a staircase. "We done already got the room and the key," Daniel explained. "All ya hafta do is unpack what ya need for tonight and take a little nap before supper."

"Thank you for taking care of me," she said. "One thing I'd better do is hang up my wedding dress. The poor thing probably looks a fright."

"You leave that dress of yours to me," said Mrs. Weaver. "I'll have it ready for the ceremony, don't worry."

"Ma's real good with a needle and thread too," Daniel informed her. "She and my sisters-in-law, Charity and Samijo? They all make dresses and hats and sell 'em in Aunt Betsy's mercantile. My other sister-in-law Bella makes coats and real fancy dresses."

"And does she sell them at the mercantile too?" Ebba asked. Her confidence in her own sewing skills slipped a notch at his words.

"Sure does. In fact, Bella makes her dresses so fancy, women from other towns come here to buy 'em."

Ebba looked away as they reached her room and Daniel unlocked the door. "I'd love to see some of them."

"Don't worry," Mrs. Weaver said. "You will."

Ebba forced a smile. She hoped his sisters-in-law weren't the competitive type. From what she'd heard so far, they didn't sound the sort. But one never knew until one actually met the person. She pushed the thought aside as she suddenly realized something. "Where do your brothers and sisters-in-law live?"

"On the farm," his mother said. "Where else?"

"You mean…you all live in the same house?!"

"'Course not," Daniel said with a laugh. "Can ya imagine all the noise?"

Ebba glanced at his mother as if to confirm his statement. "Where do they live?"

"On the farm, just like I said," Mrs. Weaver indeed confirmed. "Arlan and Samijo got their own place and so do Calvin and Bella. Only Benjamin and Charity are in the main house with Daniel and me."

Ebba's mouth twisted up into a crooked smile. "How many brothers did you say you had?"

"Just the three," Daniel replied. "But they're more than enough…"

Ma Weaver ushered them into the room. "Never mind about that. Where's that dress of yours?"

Ebba opened her mouth to speak and gasped instead. "Good gracious! Where is my bag?"

"Right there on the floor by the bed," Daniel pointed. "Did you have Harlan take care of it, Ma?"

"Sure did. Told him to give it to the hotel clerk and have it brought to the room. Now, your dress?"

Ebba hurried to comply. She hefted the bag onto the bed, opened it and pulled out her wedding dress. She shook it a few times and grimaced at the wrinkles.

"Don't worry about how it looks now," Mrs. Weaver said. "I'll fix whatever needs fixing and get it ironed and ready. My, but that's a beautiful dress."

"Thank you. Mrs. Pettigrew gave it to me."

"The lady who owns the bridal agency?" Mrs. Weaver asked.

"Yes. When she found out I didn't have one she was kind enough to give this to me. I believe it belonged to her."

Mrs. Weaver studied the garment. "It's not really a wedding dress, but it can definitely be used as one."

"Anything is better than what I had, ma'am. Which was nothing."

"All I can say is Mrs. Pettigrew must be a very generous woman to part with such a frock," Mrs. Weaver stated as she brushed at the skirt. "This is some fine material. Just look at the intricate stitching."

Ebba watched the woman admire Mrs. Pettigrew's gift. The gown was white and ivory with elbow-length sleeves trimmed in lace. Five big bows ran down the front of the bodice. Her benefactor had even given her a pearl necklace to wear with it. "You are right, Mrs. Weaver, Mrs. Pettigrew is very generous." *If a little odd,* she thought to herself. "I don't know what I would've done if she had not given me this."

"We'd have found you something, though nothing like this," she said. "Just wait until Bella sees it. She'll be green with envy!"

"Yeah," Daniel agreed. "Then she'll wanna make one just like it."

"She will?" Ebba asked in surprise.

"For the challenge, mostly," Mrs. Weaver said. She stopped fussing with the dress and turned to her. "Now I want you to do me a big favor."

"What's that?" Ebba asked.

"From now on I want you to call me Ma."

Ebba smiled and blushed. "All right… Ma."

"There now—that wasn't so hard, was it?"

Ebba shook her head. "No." She looked away, surprised at the tears in her eyes.

"What's wrong, child?" Ma asked.

"I'm sorry…it's just that I recently lost my parents. They haven't been gone for very long."

Without warning Ma pulled her into a hug. "Well now, if you need to let loose some tears you go right ahead. It isn't easy losing your parents. Daniel and his brothers know that. They lost their pa quite a while ago, but we all still miss him something fierce."

"Ma's right," Daniel agreed. "I miss him all the time. There's no shame in missin' yers."

That did it. The tears spilled down Ebba's cheeks as Ma's arms tightened around her. "I'm so sorry… I don't know where this is coming from…"

"Of course you do, child. Who wouldn't be crying? Your parents are gone, you've come West to start a whole new life, you met a passel of new people as soon as you got here and you're plumb tuckered out. Land sakes, I'm surprised the waterworks didn't start hours ago!"

"Maybe I oughta leave the room," Daniel turned toward the door.

"We'll both leave so you can rest," Ma said. "If you need us we'll be down at the mercantile. I'll send Daniel to fetch you come suppertime."

As Ma let her go, Ebba wiped at her tears. "Thank you, Ma. You too, Mr. Weaver."

"Don't ya think ya oughta be callin' me Daniel? We're gonna be married in a couple of days."

Ebba started at the comment. "A couple of days? I thought we were getting married tomorrow."

"Heavens no!" said Ma. "Not unless you want to get hitched in the dark."

"Dark? What do you mean, in the dark?" Ebba asked.

Daniel chuckled nervously. "I did tell ya in my letters where we lived, didn't I?"

"Only that you lived outside of town. You never said where exactly."

Ma put her hands on her hips and eyed him. "You mean you didn't tell her how far out?"

"I said outside of town," Daniel protested.

"How far?" Ebba asked cautiously.

"A full day's ride," Ma said. "Sunup to sundown. Two days if the weather is bad."

Ebba's legs went weak and she sat down on the bed, hard. "Two days?"

"It ain't as bad as it sounds," Daniel replied lamely.

Oh yes it is! she thought to herself. A sudden vision of never seeing another living soul crashed down upon her. Would she go crazy seeing the same handful of people day in and day out with no other social interaction? "I... I did not expect this. I thought you were maybe a mile or two out of town, not a day or two."

Ma sat next to her on the bed. "Now, it's not as bad as all that. Charity and Bella and Samijo were all from big cities and they adjusted fine. In fact, they like it better."

"Two days," Ebba muttered.

"Well, if you keep thinking about it that way, then of course it's going to bother you," Ma chastised.

Ebba closed her eyes and shook her head. "I'm sorry, it's just not what I expected. I'm sure the farm is wonderful."

"You know what's even more wonderful?" Daniel asked.

"What?" Ebba said.

"Ya ain't coughed or sneezed since ya drank Ma's remedy."

Ebba stared at him in shock. Good heavens, the man was right! Now that she thought about it, even her throat felt better. Had this tiny woman been able to do what no doctor in Denver, Chicago or New York could? "Thank you!" Ebba enthused and threw her arms around Ma. "It's a miracle!"

"No, it's just an old recipe." Ma said. "The miracle will be getting all the wrinkles out of that dress of yours." She pried Ebba's arms off and stood. "Now you get some rest. I want my new daughter-in-law to be pretty as a picture on her wedding day! And I'm sure Daniel does too, don't you, son?"

"I think she's pretty as a picture now, Ma," he said. "In fact, I think Miss Knudsen here'd look pretty no matter where or what she was doin'."

Ebba felt her cheeks grow hot with the compliment. "Thank you… Daniel."

He closed the distance between them and took her hand in his. "Rest now," he said gently. "The last thing

I'd want is for ya to start coughin' durin' our ceremony."

Ebba's heart sank. Did he have to say that? She'd
thought of it so often during her long journey West
that she'd exhausted every horrid scenario she could
possibly think of. Now she'd probably dream about it,
and whatever nightmares she had would be stuck in her
head when they stood before the preacher. "I'll do my
best," she said. And hoped her best would be enough.

Chapter Six

A soft knock sounded at the door. Ebba opened her eyes slowly, not sure if she'd heard anything.

No, there it was again. Ebba sat up, unsure of where she was. The room wasn't her own, unrecognizable...

"Miss Knudsen...er, I mean, Ebba?" came a male voice from the other side of the door.

Daniel! Now she remembered where she was. Hurriedly she got up, smoothed out the wrinkles in her skirt and answered the door.

Daniel stood there with a big smile on his face. "Did ya get a nice rest in?"

She nodded. "Maybe too nice. I forgot where I was."

He smiled. "So long as ya didn't forget me."

Ebba blushed. "No, I certainly didn't."

"Aunt Betsy has supper about ready, so Ma figured I'd best come fetch ya. Are ya hungry?"

Before she could respond verbally, her stomach growled. Her hand flew to her belly. "Oh my goodness!"

"I'll take that as a yes," he laughed.

She laughed too. "Give me a moment. I must look a mess."

He sobered. "I don't think so. I think…well, shucks, yer about the prettiest thing I've ever seen, if'n ya don't mind me sayin' so."

His words sent a tingle up her spine. "No, I, I don't mind at all."

His eyes brightened at her words. "Take all the time ya need, then. I'll be waitin' right here."

She smiled, turned and hurried to freshen up. Somewhat—really, there wasn't much she could do other than retrieve a comb out of her traveling bag, run it through her hair, twist it into a knot at the back of her head and re-pin it. But it was better than nothing. She returned to the door. "I'm ready."

"It's gettin' a little chilly outside," he informed her. "Do ya have a shawl?"

She nodded, ducked back into the room, grabbed her shawl and returned. "Now I'm really ready," she said with a smile.

"Not quite." He took her shawl from her and wrapped it around her shoulders. "There, now ya are." He offered her his arm. "Let's go."

She took it as warmth crept its way up her back. It made her whole body relax. For some reason, she wasn't nervous like she'd been at the restaurant or when the stage first pulled into town. There was something calming about the man walking next to her. She didn't know what, but she liked it.

"Aunt Betsy made roast chicken with mashed 'taters," he said. "She's almost as good a cook as Ma."

"Sounds wonderful," she said as they descended the stairs to the hotel lobby.

"You cook, right?"

"Yes, of course."

"I'm sure Ma'll teach ya all my favorites."

For some reason, she felt irritated at his words. Maybe she'd like to stand on her own two feet when it came to her cooking. In fact, many had given her high praise for it, especially when it came to traditional Swedish dishes like *fläskpannkaka*. Of course, she wasn't sure what Daniel or his family would think of a pancake full of diced pork, but was sure that's what they'd call it. Most folks had a hard time pronouncing the actual name.

She decided to take the high road. "I'd be happy to have her teach me. I can teach her too."

He gave her a sideways glance. "Ya can't teach Ma much she don't already know."

That stung. She stopped. *"Åh? Så din mamma talar svenska?"*

Daniel's mouth flopped open. "What…what was that?"

"Svenska," she said proudly. "Swedish."

He gaped at her a moment before he looked her up and down. "Ya speak another language? Well, woo-ee! Ain't that somethin'?"

His excitement took her by surprise. *"Ja."*

He grinned ear to ear. "Say somethin' else."

She shrugged. *"Vad är för* dessert?"

"Dessert? Is that a Swedish word?" he asked.

"No, English."

"Oh. Bella sometimes mixes English words in with her Eye-talian."

Ebba smiled at his pronunciation and tried not to laugh.

"What did ya say before that?"

"Before what?"

"Before what ya just said?"

"Oh, I said, 'so, your mother speaks Swedish?'"

His smiled faded. "Oh. I guess yer right—ya *could* teach her too. Ma don't speak nothin' but good ol' English. Better'n I do, at least."

Ebba noted the look on his face and wondered if she'd hurt his feelings. He obviously loved his mother very much. "We can teach each other different things."

"Yeah, we can," he agreed. His smile returned. "We'd better get a move on before Ma sends Matty to come look for us."

They didn't speak much the rest of their walk to the mercantile. Just as well—so far they'd both managed to embarrass the other through their own pride, the focus on his mother. She liked Mary Weaver, and didn't want to do anything to make her start feeling differently about her.

By the time they reached their destination, supper was ready and on the table. "About time you two got here," Ma said as they came into the kitchen.

"There you are," added his Aunt Betsy. "Now everyone grab a seat and we'll get started with the introductions. Then your uncle can say the blessing."

Everyone sat. Ebba noticed three empty chairs but kept quiet. Within moments a young couple came into the kitchen followed by Daniel's uncle. As soon as they were seated, she gave them a smile and a nod of greeting.

"Matthew, Charlotte, this is your cousin Daniel's mail-order bride." Aunt Betsy motioned toward her. "Ava, is it? No, that's not right…"

"Eh-bah," Ma Weaver sounded out. "Land sakes, it's only four letters. It's not that hard, Betsy."

"Well, how's a person supposed to know these things?" Betsy shot back. "It's not a name you hear around these parts."

"I think it's a lovely name," the young woman at the other end of the table said. "Allow me to introduce myself—I'm Charlotte Quinn." She reached over and patted the hand of the young man next to her. "And this is Matthew, my husband."

"You have an accent too," Ebba commented. "Where are you from?"

"Mississippi, originally, until we moved here to Nowhere."

"I like the way you talk," she said. "It's very pretty."

"Why, thank you. I have had a few people comment about my accent before, but no woman has ever told me it was pretty."

"They may have been jealous, dear," Matthew said. "It's so nice to meet you at last, Ebba. And if no one else has told you yet, welcome to the family."

"Thank you. This is a little overwhelming for me.

Everything and everyone is so new. You'll excuse me if I don't remember everyone's name."

Daniel and his mother exchanged a quick glance then did the same with Charlotte and Matthew. What was that about?

Daniel's uncle gave Ebba a nod. "In case anyone is wondering, I'm Lancaster Quinn and I'll second what Matthew said. Welcome to the family, Ebba."

"Thank you so much." She glanced around the table. "Is this all of you? Are there any more?"

"This is all of us as far as the Quinn family goes," Aunt Betsy said. "But when you get out to the farm… ow!" She glared at Ma next to her. "What was that for?"

Ma gave her an innocent glance. "What? I didn't do anything."

"You kicked me!"

"If I did, it was an accident. Now let's get on with supper—can't you see the poor child is starving?"

Daniel covered his mouth and tried not to laugh. Ebba watched him and wondered why his mother would kick his aunt in the first place. There was something they weren't telling her, and it made her nervous.

But she pushed the thought from her mind as Daniel's uncle folded his hands in front of him and bowed his head. "Dear Lord, for what we are about to receive, may we be truly thankful. Oh, and thank you for sending such a nice bride for my nephew, and may the two of them be very happy together. Amen."

Everyone raised their head. "Not so fast," Ma Weaver said. "I want to add a few words."

"A few words?" Aunt Betsy said with a frown. "Don't take all night, or the food will get cold."

Ma looked like she was about to kick her sister again, but instead bowed her head. "Lord, you know how long poor Daniel's been waiting for a bride. Just put in him the patience needed so he can get to know her a little better before he makes her an honest woman."

"Ma!" Daniel blurted as his face turned red.

"Well it's only natural, son. For Heaven's sake, at least learn a little bit about each other before you—"

"Aunt Mary," Matthew interrupted. "Not at the supper table."

"Shucks, Matty," Daniel said. "She says things like this at our table all the time."

Ebba sat, her cheeks flushed. Were they talking about what she thought they were?

Charlotte's eyes widened as she stared at Daniel, then his mother. "You do?!"

"Well, dagnabit, what's wrong with it?" Ma asked. "It's nature. No need to hide it."

Ebba started to fan herself with one hand. "I hear you make a good roast chicken, Mrs. Quinn," she said in hopes of changing the subject.

Betsy took the cue. "Oh yes, I'm quite proud of my recipe. Do you cook well, Ebba?"

"I like to think so," she said. "I make a combination of American and Swedish recipes."

"Did you grow up here in America, or come over to this country as a child?" Charlotte asked as she reached for the mashed potatoes. She cast a cautious glance in Ma's direction.

"I was raised here, but I lived with my parents and their extended family—aunts, uncles, cousins. I was the youngest."

"And where are all of your relatives now?" Matthew asked.

Ebba fixed her eyes on her plate. "Gone."

"Gone?" Aunt Betsy repeated. "What do you mean, they're gone?"

"They are all dead. Could you please pass me the chicken?" she asked Daniel.

He reached for the platter and offered it to her. "I remember ya tellin' me yer parents had both passed, but I had no idea ya didn't have another livin' relative to speak of."

She stabbed a piece of chicken with a fork and put it on her plate. "My parents were all that was left. Most of the family died from influenza about five years ago." She pointed at a dish of carrots. "Could you pass that, please?"

Ma Weaver passed her the vegetables. "You poor child. All alone in the world."

"Not anymore she's not," Daniel said. "Once ya become my wife, then trust me, you'll never be alone again."

"That's the truth," Ma said with a tiny smile. "Now let's eat. We've got a long day ahead of us tomorrow."

The rest of the evening was spent in comfortable conversation with the Quinns, Daniel and his mother. Matthew and Charlotte regaled her with tales of their own courtship and subsequent wedding. She listened attentively and tried not to cringe. To think that they got all the way to the altar and practically at the "I do's" before the deputy Sheriff Hughes had told her about stopped the ceremony and switched brides with Matthew. It was all too fantastic to take in! "You could write a book!" she said at the end of the tale.

"If there's any story writing, it will be done by Deputy Turner," Matthew said. "He's the town storyteller."

"Storyteller?" Ebba said.

"Yep, ol' Tom's a master at spinnin' yarns," Daniel said. "I can't tell ya how many times he's had me sittin' on the edge of my seat. Me and a whole lotta other people."

Ebba smiled and wondered if she should say anything about the sheriff's plan to lure Deputy Turner back to Clear Creek. No—that was the sheriff's business and she should be quiet about it. "It was a wonderful story. Thank you for sharing it with me."

"It's definitely something we'll be telling our children one day," Matthew said.

Ebba studied him. He had an odd look on his face she wondered about. But again, not her business. "And your grandchildren," she added.

Mrs. Quinn drummed her fingers on the kitchen table a few times. "Anyone ready for dessert?" Within moments the woman had served everyone a cup of coffee and a piece of pie. A very small piece, Ebba noticed.

Apparently, she wasn't the only one that did. "What are you trying to do, Betsy?" Ma asked. "Are you rationing the pie now?"

Aunt Betsy made a show of giving each man a solemn glare. "Perhaps it's on account of half my pie having gone missing sometime this afternoon."

Ma glanced at each of the men herself. "I've had that same thing happen at my place. Funny business, that. Mouse traps work. Wonderful invention, mouse traps—can't say as I could get along without 'em."

Daniel's eyes widened. He nodded nervously. "They sure 'nough do, Ma."

"You ought to know," she replied with a smirk.

Matthew openly grimaced. "No mouse traps, Mother, please?"

"What's the matter, Matty?" Daniel asked. "Where's yer sense of adventure?"

"I need my hands for work," he stated then smiled at his mother.

"That goes for me too," Mr. Quinn volunteered. "You wouldn't want Matthew and I unable to do our jobs, would you?"

"All I know is that if you boys don't stop eating half a pie every afternoon, I'm going to stop baking them!" Aunt Betsy warned.

"Now there's a clear threat if'n I ever heard one," Daniel said in awe. "Me, I'd rather face the mouse traps than live without pie."

"If we don't stop flapping our gums," his mother said, "we'll never get a chance to enjoy what little we have in front of us."

Ebba laughed. "All of this over pie?"

"Pie is serious business in this house," Betsy stated. "And just as serious at my sister's."

Ebba smiled at Ma. "I won't steal your pie."

"I'm sure you won't, child. Which is why I'll have you help me set the traps."

Daniel groaned. "I ain't even married yet and Ma's turning my wife against me!"

Ebba laughed again. Daniel joined her and together they started to eat their pie.

The next morning Ebba awoke at the crack of dawn. Or rather, Ma Weaver woke her by banging on her door. "Time to get going, Ebba girl! Let's not waste daylight! Do what you have to do, gather your things and meet me downstairs!"

Ebba sat up, stretched and yawned. She'd slept like the dead—she hadn't realized how tired she was. Of course, all the laughing last night had helped relax her. She realized that she'd never shared such laughter before, not even with her own family. It felt good, and she was eager to share it again. She hoped the opportunity presented itself during that day, or at the very least, that night.

She got out of bed, washed her face, dressed and ran a comb through her hair, then quickly braided it. She began to hum as she wrapped the braid around her head and pinned it in place. Gathering her things, she noticed her wedding dress wasn't there and almost panicked before remembering Ma had taken it the day before to try and fix it for the wedding. She sighed in relief.

Then the unwanted thought returned: would there *be* a wedding? Would her allergies be an insurmountable barrier? What good would fixing the dress do if she was just going to stuff it back into her bag again? She hoped she wouldn't have to find out, but…

Downstairs, Ma was waiting with Aunt Betsy. "Do you have all your things, child?"

"Yes. Do you still have my dress?"

"Of course, dear—I've taken care of it."

"It's a shame you already have a dress," Aunt Betsy said. "I just love helping a bride get ready for her wedding! So does Leona, Sheriff Hughes's sister. But maybe we could come a day early. Mary, what do you think?"

"There's no need for that," Ma said. "This poor child will have enough to worry about without the two of you fussing over her."

"Fussing?" Ebba said. "Why would they be fussing?"

"On account so many people are coming to the wedding," Ma said. "Land sakes, I think half the town will be there at this point."

Ebba's eyes went wide as platters. What was she saying? "Half the town? But I thought it would be too far away?"

"That's what I thought too," Ma remarked calmly. "But it seems lots of people are willing to make the trip. Let's see, there's the Rileys—you know, Leona and her family—the Johnsons, the Turners, Harlan… I mean, Sheriff Hughes…now who else?"

Ebba could only stare. "There's more?" Well, she supposed it really didn't matter how many people attended their wedding. After all, they *were* friends of the family—of course they would want to see Daniel married. "That's not so bad."

Aunt Betsy chuckled. "That's because there's only so many places for folks to camp out."

Ebba glanced nervously between the two women. She wasn't even going to comment on that one. Better to wait and find out for herself when the time came. Until then, she planned on enjoying the trip to what she hoped would be her new home.

Chapter Seven

When Ma said the trip to the farm would take an entire day, she wasn't exaggerating. It was dark before they arrived, and Ebba had no idea how the horses found their way the last couple of miles. Lots of practice, maybe? Whatever it was, she was glad for it. Her backside was killing her. They didn't even stop at the Gundersons' for lunch, though Daniel explained that was their usual routine. But he and his mother wanted to get home, and that was that.

The one stop they did make was near a pond to rest at midday. It was a beautiful spot and Ebba hoped she could go back there someday. She suspected they skipped the Gundersons' just to be able to picnic for an hour under the big willow tree near the water. Ma explained that Charity and Benjamin had fallen in love with each other in that very spot.

It was all Ebba could do not to scorn the romantic notion, because to her, that was all it was. How could two people fall in love that quickly? Mail-order brides didn't marry for love, they married to survive. That was why she became one. She certainly hoped Daniel realized that, and that it might take her some time to feel any sort of affection for him.

But apparently such was not the case with his brothers and their wives. They seemed to fall in love just by tripping over one another or being in the same room, if one believed Ma. Ebba didn't, and worried that Daniel might.

Truth be told, she hadn't planned to fall in love at all. In fact, she'd convinced herself there might be no such thing in her marriage with Daniel. Convenience had a way of dampening romance. She liked him and his mother so far, and the townspeople (okay, the Quinns and Sheriff Hughes) spoke highly of them. But only time would tell.

Mrs. Pettigrew, on the other hand, believed in love at first sight. She'd gone on about it at length when Ebba dropped by the bridal agency to get her train ticket, even though the Pettigrew Bridal Agency had sent out only two brides so far. Ebba made three, and the third time wasn't always the charm.

Ebba hoped to fall in love with her husband one day. But she wasn't counting on it happening tomorrow or the next day, or the next month for all of that. Maybe in the years to come. Her parents had taught her there was no such thing as instant romance.

"Whoa," Daniel called to the horses as he brought the team to a stop. Ebba studied the two-story farmhouse in the darkness. A light shone downstairs, and two of the windows upstairs were also aglow. "Ma,

Ebba, why don't ya go inside and I'll bring everythin' in?" Daniel suggested.

"I'll get Benjamin to come out and help you," his mother said. "Come on, Ebba—I'll show you to your room."

Daniel helped his mother out of the wagon first, then reached up to help Ebba. His hands were warm and she shivered at his touch. She was curious about the tingling sensations he caused and wondered why she would feel them. No one else had ever caused them. Was it because she thought he was attractive? The idea was sobering. And he'd said he thought she was…

"Thank you," she told him as her feet touched the ground.

"Go on in, sweetie. Ma'll show you around, and ya can meet Benjamin and Charity."

Ma was already standing in the doorway. "Listen to the man, child. Follow me." She turned and went inside.

Ebba did the same. She closed the door after she entered, studied her surroundings and found she liked the rugged warmth of the house. This was a home, no doubt about it. None of the tenements she'd lived in had ever felt or looked like this. There was a parlor to her left, a dining room to her right. She didn't see anyone in either and wondered where the rest of the family was.

The answer came in the sound of heavy footsteps descending the staircase. "Is that you, Ma?"

Ebba smiled as a man reached the bottom. She could see the resemblance between Daniel and his older brother and wondered if this was one of the twins. Or perhaps Arlan, the oldest—Ma had explained to her that he visited the main farmhouse a lot with his wife Samijo. Best to let him introduce himself, lest she make a mistake.

"Oh, you're not Ma. So you must be Ebba—did I say it right?"

Ebba smiled brightly. "Yes, you did, thank you."

"I'm Benjamin, Daniel's big brother." He held out his hand.

She took it and gave it a healthy shake. "It's nice to meet you, Benjamin. Your brother and mother have told me a lot about you."

"Just stick with the good parts and forget the rest. I'm sure the rest was real bad."

"Not as bad as you would think," she said with a smile.

"The look on yer face tells me it was," he said slyly. "Ma must be in the kitchen. Ya want some coffee?"

"Thank you, I'd love some. It was a long ride out here."

"Don't I know! I've done that trip all my life."

She followed him into the kitchen and found Ma already putting things away. She glanced around, wondering where Daniel was. She hadn't seen him come in through the front door.

Then he walked in from the back, his arms loaded with packages. "Howdy, Benjamin," he said with a grin. "Have ya met my bride?"

"Sure have—and I must say, ya got yerself a pretty one!"

Ebba felt herself blush once again—this was getting

to be a habit! She really didn't know what to say, but thankfully no one was expecting her to say anything.

"Let me get ya that coffee." Benjamin went to the stove, picked up the pot and shook it to make sure it wasn't empty. "Good, Calvin didn't drink it all." He went to a hutch, took out a cup and saucer, set them on the table, poured her a cup and motioned to a chair. "Make yerself at home. Daniel and I'll bring yer things in from the wagon."

She did as he suggested and sat. Considering the state of her derrière, she would rather have stood, but thought it would be impolite. She sipped her coffee and let the hot brew warm her. Even though it was June, the nights were still chilly. Another hour of riding in the wagon and she'd have been frozen to the bone. She didn't have a coat anymore; the only outer garment she owned was that shawl.

It didn't take long for Daniel and Benjamin to bring in the rest of her luggage and the supplies. Soon they had them put away and were sitting at the table with her. "I can't think what might be keepin' Charity," Benjamin finally said. "I'd best go upstairs and check on her. I know she's anxious to meet ya—she's been talkin' 'bout it all day."

"She has?" Ebba said. "But… I am a stranger to her."

"Stranger?" Ma said in surprise. "You're no stranger, child. In a couple of days you're going to be family. Stop thinking like that."

Ebba glanced at each of them. "I'm afraid I'm not

used to the idea yet. I haven't had any family for a long time. You'll pardon me if it takes time for me to adjust."

"Shucks, sweetie, we understand," Daniel said sympathetically. "Don't ya worry, before ya know it you'll be actin' just like the rest of us. A Weaver through and through."

Benjamin coughed into his hand in an attempt to stifle a chuckle. One escaped anyway.

"Benjamin," Ma said. "Mind your manners!"

"Sure, Ma," he said with a smile. He looked at Ebba. "I'm only laughin' because I know ya ain't sure what 'bein' a Weaver through and through' means. If ya did, ya'd be laughin' too."

Ebba could only stare for a moment before her face broke into a smile. "I think I'm looking forward to finding out. I think."

"Think what?" a woman asked as she entered the kitchen.

"There ya are!" Benjamin declared. "Ebba, this is my wife Charity. Charity, meet Ebba."

"Aww," Daniel said with a frown. "I was gonna introduce her."

"Well, then be quicker next time, li'l brother." Benjamin smacked him on the back of the head.

"Boys…" Ma warned. "Try to behave like gentlemen. Just because we're home doesn't mean you have to act like a bunch of miscreants."

Ebba did her best to suppress a giggle.

"Don't laugh," Daniel said with as much seriousness as he could muster. "Even though we're grown, she can still take a switch to us."

"He's right," Charity agreed. "I've seen her do it myself."

Ebba blanched and quickly looked the petite Mrs. Weaver up and down in awe. "You mean you've... struck them?"

"Land sakes, child, I can't count how many times I've given them a good hiding. Somebody's gotta do it, even if they don't seem to take the hint. Is there any coffee left?"

Benjamin retrieved another cup and saucer, poured his mother some coffee and handed it to her. "Here ya go, Ma—this'll warm ya up. Did ya want Charity to get a bath ready for ya?"

"I'm not the one that needs a hot soak right now— that would be poor Ebba here. Who knows when she had one last?"

"It...has been a while," Ebba said in embarrassment.

"Charity, Benjamin, go get a bath ready for her, then show her to her room. Me, I'm going upstairs to get ready for bed myself. Making that ride in one day is hard on a body, especially one my age."

"Are ya gonna be all right, Ma?" Daniel asked with concern.

"Sure, Danny," she said. "I'm just not as young as I used to be. Now go take care of the horses and wagon. And remember, Ebba's going to be sleeping in your room tonight, so that means you're in the barn."

"Aw, Ma, I know that," he said as he headed for the back door.

Ebba watched him go and felt herself smile. This was a close-knit family, a family that loved each other.

Not that her own family hadn't, but they didn't get along as well as the Weavers. She turned to Charity and Benjamin. "I would love a bath, but you don't have to get it ready for me. I'm perfectly capable of doing it myself."

"Consider it a welcoming gift," Charity said. "Trust me, later on you'll have plenty of work to do."

Ebba nodded in understanding. With this many people in the house, of course she would. She knew Charity and Benjamin had at least one child. She couldn't remember how many more there were—she'd lost track somewhere between the Gundersons' and here, but she knew it was quite a few. But a house was happier when it was full of children.

She smiled at the thought, sat back and took another sip of coffee. Yes, she was home.

The next day Ebba awoke with a start, again unable to remember where she was for a moment. "Oh my goodness," she said in shock, "I'm getting married!" She glanced around the room, then mumbled, "I am getting married, aren't I?" As she recalled, no one told her exactly when the wedding would be, though they'd hinted it might be today. But that was before half of Nowhere had decided to attend...

Oh good grief, she thought to herself. Well, whenever it was, she hoped she'd be ready for it.

She climbed out of bed, washed her face, combed her hair and got dressed, then went downstairs. She belatedly remembered that Daniel had slept in the barn because she had his room. She hoped he wasn't too cold last night and thought she'd find him in the kitchen warming himself. But the only one there was Charity, frying potatoes at the stove. "Good morning," the other woman called.

"Good morning. Have you seen Daniel yet?"

"No, I haven't. He and the other men are doing their morning chores."

"How long does that usually take?"

"Not long. A couple of hours, give or take."

"A couple of hours? What kind of chores are they doing?"

Charity shrugged. "The usual—feed the stock, milk the cow, gather eggs, clean the barn, maybe start the plowing…"

"All before breakfast?" Ebba interrupted.

"All before breakfast," Charity echoed with a smile. "What kind of chores did you have?"

Ebba slipped into a chair. "I lived in the city all my life." She thought a moment. "I've done my fair share of laundry, dishes and keeping house, but that's about it. There was no egg gathering or plowing involved. We simply went to the corner market."

"Ah yes, I'm familiar with that. I grew up in a small town—not as big as where you're from, but bigger than Nowhere."

"Did it take you a long time? To adjust to living on a farm?"

Charity shrugged again as she stirred her potatoes. "Not as long as I thought it would. Besides, it's not like we're out there plowing the fields with the men. At least not yet."

"Not yet? You mean I'm going to have to plow?" Ebba asked in shock.

"No, silly. But sometimes we do go out and remove rocks. It depends on the ground they're trying to work."

Ebba sat back in her chair and blew out her breath. "I had no idea one had to remove rocks."

"If the fields are full of them and you want to grow something there, that's what you have to do," Charity stated. "But don't let me make it sound like you're going to be pulling the plow yourself. And so far I haven't had to pick up a single rock. Bella's picked up a few," she added.

"Bella?"

"Isabella, Calvin's wife. Don't tell me no one told you about Bella?"

"No, they told me. I've just never heard of a woman who would voluntarily go out and pick rocks up. It seems unladylike."

Charity shook her head. "This is a farm, Ebba. We do what we have to do to make it work. Including right here in this kitchen. Would you mind slicing the bread for me?"

"Not at all." She got up. Two fresh-baked loaves were cooling on a worktable, and a knife lay nearby.

"There's a serving platter in the hutch," Charity said. "You can use that."

Ebba went to the hutch, opened it, found the platter and returned to the worktable to slice the bread. "When will I meet Bella and the others?"

"You'll meet some of them at breakfast. Arlan and Samijo sometimes join us. I made extra this morning

because I figured they'd want to meet the new arrival."
Charity winked. "Whoever's coming should be here
any minute."

Ebba finished her slicing, set the platter of bread
on the table, then tried to smooth her skirt. She suddenly felt nervous at the thought of meeting more of
Daniel's family. Truth be told, she was still trying to
get over how much more family was here than she'd
been led to believe.

She'd no sooner thought it than a tall man opened
the kitchen's back door and stepped inside, two small
boys in his arms. Ebba gasped. "Twins!"

Charity and the man both laughed. "There's no
shortage of that around here," he said. He set both
boys on their feet and they immediately ran to Charity for a hug.

"They're adorable!" Ebba said with a smile. "What
are their names?"

"Justin and Jason," he said.

Ebba studied them. "How on Earth do you tell them
apart?"

"Justin has the clouded eye," a woman said as she
came through the back door.

Ebba turned to her and noted the baby girl in her
arms. She couldn't be more than a year old. "You must
be Samijo?" She hoped she was pronouncing it cor-
rectly.

"And you must be Ebba." The woman balanced the
child on one hip and held out her hand.

Ebba shook it. "And whom might this be?" she
asked, pointing to the babe.

"This is Autumn, our youngest. Did you sleep well?"

"Well enough to forget where I was this morning," Ebba said with a laugh. She peeked past Samijo through the open door. "When will the others come in?"

"They're headin' this way now," the man said, then offered her his hand. "I'm Arlan, in case you ain't figgered it out yet."

"It's nice to meet you," Ebba said politely. "I understand you and Samijo have a cabin across one of the orchards."

"That's right," Samijo said. "After we get some things taken care of I'll show it to you. We'll have to go over there anyway to start the baking."

"Baking?" Ebba said.

"Yes, for your wedding," Charity chimed in. "We've got a lot of pies to make between now and then."

Ebba could feel her cheeks grow hot. "Er…when exactly…is the wedding?"

Everyone looked at her, their mouths half-open, before they glanced at each other. "I thought it was tomorrow," Arlan said.

"No, that can't be right," Samijo told him. "I think it's the day after tomorrow."

"You probably don't know this yet, but a lot of people in town are planning to come," Charity replied. "It'll likely be in a few days."

"Land sakes, doesn't anybody listen to anyone around here?" Ma barked as she entered the kitchen. "Samijo was right—it's the day after tomorrow. There's too much work to be done and folks can't get here that fast. We had to plan on an extra day."

"So we have two days to get ready." Charity crossed her arms in front of her. "Who's in charge of the main meal? Did you tell those invited to bring something, Ma?"

"Betsy and Charlotte are bringing bread," Ma informed her. "Leona and her girls are bringing the fruits and vegetables. We're making the cake and the pies."

"What about the meat?" Samijo asked.

"Mr. Davis is bringing a pig."

"A…pig?" Ebba asked in surprise.

"Yes, isn't it wonderful?" Ma said. "That pig will feed everyone and then some. We can roast it right in the barnyard."

"Roast it?" Ebba squeaked. "You mean it will be… *alive* when he gets here?"

"Not for long," Arlan chuckled.

Ebba fell onto the nearest chair. "Oh dear. The poor pig."

"I bet you never said 'poor pig' when you bought pork chops at the butcher shop in Denver," Ma said as she went to the hutch and got herself a cup and saucer.

"I never thought about it," Ebba said with a grimace. "Maybe because we didn't buy much meat."

"If you're squeamish about such things," Ma said, "then make yourself scarce when Mr. Davis does the deed."

"The…deed?" Ebba swallowed hard.

"Good grief, child, you're white as a sheet!" Ma quickly set the cup and saucer in front of her, went to the stove and grabbed the coffee pot. After pouring Ebba a cup she went back to the hutch for more cups and saucers and served up the rest of the pot. "Charity, we'll have to make another."

"Right away, Ma," Charity said, then froze as a sudden wail from upstairs caught everyone's attention. "Never mind—Truly's awake. Samijo, will you do the honors?"

"Sure, I don't mind." Samijo reached for the empty pot.

"I'll be right back." Charity left the kitchen and headed for the staircase.

Ebba sat as Samijo and Ma picked up where Charity had left off with breakfast. She had to admit, the women were like a finely tuned machine as they worked together. She just hoped she didn't do anything to mess up the gears.

Chapter Eight

Breakfast was a boisterous affair complete with crying children, a barking dog and lots of laughter between Daniel, Arlan and Benjamin. Ebba had yet to meet Calvin, Benjamin's twin, and wondered when he and Bella would come by the house. Ma told her that they usually ate in their own home, which had been completed last year. It had taken the men quite a while to get it built, what with having a farm to run, but they'd managed to help their brother out.

"It must be a large house for it to take so long to build," Ebba said.

"It's big, all right," Arlan agreed. "Come to think of it, about as big as this place."

"How many bedrooms does it have?" Ebba asked.

"Four, same as this one," Ma said. "The good Lord knows they need the room."

"Four bedrooms?" Ebba said in surprise. "Are they planning on having a lot of children?"

"Planning?" Benjamin said with a laugh. "Too late for that!"

Ebba glanced around the table, confused, and noted everyone had the same amused expression. "Did they have…triplets?"

Daniel, who was seated next to her, flew into a fit of laughter. "No, darlin', they ain't got triplets. Not that that couldn't happen, 'specially in this family!"

"I could be so lucky," Ma said. "But I have enough on my hands as it is with the ones we do have."

Ebba sipped her coffee, placed the cup in its saucer and glanced at Justin and Jason sitting across from her in their parents' laps. Ma held Autumn in her arms. "Four is a good number of grandchildren," she said. "They're close enough together in age so they'll grow up together and always have each other for playmates."

Everyone stared at her.

Ebba glanced around the table again. "What did I say?"

Ma smiled and looked at Benjamin. "When *is* your brother coming up to the house?"

"Pretty soon, Ma," he said. "Why?"

"I think it's time to get all the introductions over with, that's all," she said.

Daniel smiled and covered his mouth with a hand. "Yeah, I guess we'd better."

"So I will meet them before you go to work for the day?" Ebba asked.

"That's a good idea," Ma said. "We have a lot of work today too, ladies. Ebba, how are you at baking cookies?"

"I make very good cookies. At least my father thought so."

"Then you're in charge of baking those today. Samijo, what were you planning?"

"Well, I'd like to show Ebba my home, but I'm going to need my oven for pies."

"You girls can run across the orchard and take care of that after breakfast and the introductions," Ma said. "Then Ebba can come back here and start on those cookies."

Ebba was about to ask her what kind of cookies she wanted when a commotion sounded outside the kitchen door. Everyone ignored the ruckus except her. It was all she could do not to stand and look to see what was coming—it sounded like quite a crowd!

The kitchen door burst open and a small boy with dark curly hair ran in. "*Nonna!* Did ya save me any bacon?" He had the oddest accent—like a cross between the Weaver men and Mr. Milioti, the greengrocer back in Denver.

"Now you know I love you as much as the next person, Leo," Ma said, "but I'm afraid I ate all of it. Though Daniel's mail-order bride is going to bake cookies later."

The boy looked around the table, his eyes finally landing on Ebba. "Are you?" he asked and pointed at her.

"Leonardo, didn't yer ma tell ya it ain't polite to point?" Daniel asked.

The boy's hand dropped as he looked at Daniel. "Who is she?"

"Yer grandma just told ya," Daniel said. "This here's

Ebba, my mail-order bride. We're gonna get hitched in a couple days. Ya wanna come?"

Leo didn't have a chance to respond, as five more children piled in through the door, followed by the most beautiful woman Ebba had ever seen. She actually gasped at the sight of her.

Behind the woman came a man carrying an infant in one muscular arm—clearly Benjamin's brother Calvin. Ebba wouldn't have been able to tell them apart except that Calvin hadn't shaved that morning. Well, his chin was shaved, but his upper lip sported a few days' growth of hair. "Mornin', everyone!" he said happily and headed straight for Ebba with his hand extended. "I'm Calvin—I'm gonna be yer new brother-in-law!"

Ebba was about to return the greeting when a girl in her early to mid-teens came in with a baby on each hip. The girl went straight for the beauty standing next to Calvin. "Here, Bella, I changed them both for you."

"Thank you, Rufi. You are such a help to me. You will make a fine wife one day."

"Here, why don't you take Thatcher for me?" Calvin handed the toddler he was holding off to the girl.

Ebba openly gawked—she couldn't help it at this point. Children spilled into the hallway, the kitchen not big enough to hold everyone. Some ran upstairs while others went into the parlor, jumping and laughing all the way. The house was suddenly a cacophony of English seasoned heavily with Italian. Perhaps she shouldn't worry about slipping into her native Swedish now and then. But all of these children couldn't possibly belong to Calvin and Bella, could they?

"I suppose you're wondering where all these younguns came from," Ma yelled over the noise.

Ebba slowly nodded, eyes wide.

"Well, Bella's parents passed away, so after she and Calvin married, she sent for her brothers and sisters to come join them. They were staying with an aunt in New York, but her health wasn't so good. So here they are!"

Ebba continued to stare in shock at the children running here and there. Daniel reached over and put a hand over hers. "You okay, sweetie?" he asked.

His touch snapped her out of her stupor. "You… never mentioned…any of *this* in your letters!"

"What for? I figured ya were gonna meet them once ya got here anyway. I thought it'd be a nice surprise. So, ya surprised?"

She gaped at him. "I'm beyond surprised, actually. How do you feed them all?"

"Why do ya think it took us so long to build Calvin's house?" Daniel asked. "We had to plant a few extra fields to feed 'em all. But we gotta system now and it works just fine. Don't worry, sweetie, you're only one extra mouth," he added with a grin.

Ebba looked at him in horror as visions of cooking for this army of Weavers stretched before her. She looked at Ma. "Are you sure one pig at our wedding will be enough?"

Samijo guided Ebba through an orchard and across a field to her cabin. The peace and quiet was a far cry from the chaos of the farmhouse, and Ebba reveled in it.

The little valley where the farm was located was beautiful, peaceful and serene…so long as Calvin, Bella and company weren't around.

But after Samijo elaborated on why Calvin and Bella had brought her siblings to the farm, things made better sense. Ebba supposed that if she had a lot of brothers and sisters being raised by a sickly aunt, she'd have done the same thing. Bella had married an exceptional man. Most wouldn't do what Calvin Weaver had done, taking on seven of his wife's young siblings and putting them all in the same house. He'd become an instant father, of sorts, not to mention having his own children.

She shook her head. Ten children under one roof with two adults…not that such was uncommon. But it certainly wasn't easy. It was a testimony to Calvin Weaver's kind heart and generous spirit that he hadn't told his wife no.

"I think I'll make apple pies," Samijo said, pulling Ebba from her thoughts. "And maybe some peach cobbler."

"How do you get the apples? Ebba asked. "There aren't any on the trees."

Samijo stared at her a moment, then laughed. "I'm sorry, you'll have to excuse me. It's been a long time since I lived in a city. We harvest the apples in late summer. I'll use the ones we canned last year. Canned ones work better for pie anyway, I think."

Ebba glanced around the small kitchen. "I've never canned before. There was no need in the city."

"I know—I came here from New Orleans. I used to

go to the market for my uncle Burr three times a week or more." She too looked around the cabin. "Out here, though, it's a lot different. But having lived in both places, I wouldn't trade this life for ten thousand dollars."

"Ten thousand? That's a lot of money. You might think differently if someone set that much money in front of you."

Samijo smiled and turned away. "Not as hard as you might think." She went to a cupboard, opened it and pulled out several large jars. "I'll start with these, but first let me show you around. When Arlan and I were first married, the place looked very much like it does right now."

Ebba studied her surroundings. There were two chairs and a couch in the living area. The kitchen and dining area was small, but adequate for the size of their family. Two doors led into two separate bedrooms. "What will you do when you have more children? They all can't share a room forever."

"No, they can't," Samijo agreed. "Which is why we plan on adding a second story. That way we can have two more bedrooms. Justin and Jason can share one, then we'll go from there."

"I can't imagine what your brother-in-law Calvin's house is like."

"I can tell you, it's a lot more organized than you might think. I know Bella's brothers and sisters are loud and boisterous, just like the Weavers. But they're happy children, very polite, and they do as they're told. The oldest has her own room, while the boys share one and the rest of the girls another. The older kids take care of the younger ones, and Bella runs it all like an Army sergeant. It all works out."

"What about the babies?" Ebba asked.

"Alastair and Hugh are in Calvin and Bella's room right now. When they're old enough they'll go to the boys' room. Well, unless Rufina—we call her Rufi— is ready for marriage by then."

"How old is she now?"

"Sixteen and a real beauty, just like her sister— she'll have no trouble finding a husband. But there'll be trouble if he doesn't want to live here on the farm. I can't imagine any of them leaving at this point, any more than I can imagine Arlan and I would."

Ebba walked over to a chair at the table and sat. "I hope you don't mind me saying this, but I'm over-whelmed. Daniel didn't tell me anything about…" She waved a hand in the air. "…having so much family. I thought it was just him and his mother."

Samijo sat across from her. "Oh, you poor thing. I'm sorry he didn't tell you. I hope you're not too angry with him."

"I guess I am a little angry. I envisioned a nice lit-tle house with just the two of us and now I… I don't know what to think."

Samijo suddenly straightened. "You're not thinking of backing out of marrying Daniel, are you?"

"Oh no, it's just that… I'm not sure what to think of all this. If he didn't tell me about all of you, then what else hasn't he told me?"

"Daniel wouldn't lie, Ebba. Really, none of the

Weavers would, ever. I guess because he's used to having so many people around, he didn't think that you might not be as comfortable with them. At least give him a chance to apologize. But first you have to tell him how you feel."

Ebba shrugged, unsure of what to say. She didn't want to use the words *betrayed* or *cheated*, but they were how she felt. "What's done is done. It's not important anymore."

"It is if you think so. You need to tell Daniel. Trust me, you'll want to be able to tell each other anything. Arlan and I have had our quarrels over the last few years, most of which could've been avoided if we'd only talked to each other instead of shutting each other out. It's no different with Charity and Benjamin. They've had their moments."

"And what about Calvin and Bella?"

"They don't have that problem," Samijo said with a smile. "Bella speaks her mind *all* the time."

Ebba's eyes widened. But she'd met Bella, and could see the woman wasn't the type to hold anything back. "It's my guess that she takes some getting used to?"

"You guessed right, but you will. And once you do, you will love her just like we do. I wouldn't change her a bit."

"I'll take your word for it," Ebba said with a smile. "Now how can I help you?"

Ebba helped Samijo prepare some pies before heading back to the main house. Crossing the field and entering the orchard had a calming effect on her, and she stopped to note the beauty of the trees and landscape around her. She'd never been in an orchard before today and enjoyed the smells. The blossoms had long since fallen to the ground and were lost to the winds and rain, but it was nonetheless lovely.

She took a deep breath of fresh air, sighed...and sneezed. "Oh no!" she sniffed as she wiped at her nose with her hand. "Where's my handkerchief?" She patted the pockets of her skirt in vain—she must have left it at the house.

She began to sneeze again and again. "Drat!" She lifted her skirt and tried to hurry back. Maybe Ma could whip her up another batch of that concoction she'd made in town. She could certainly use some, especially now that it was late morning—her affliction would be in full force soon. Would she even be able to bake cookies? She had one task assigned to her, an easy one at that, and here she was, fighting a sneezing fit.

She did her best to stay on the path, stumbling twice because of her sneezing and almost falling over. How embarrassing would that be? Good grief, she could barely walk, her eyes were so watery. She longed to rub them, but that would only make things worse. It always did. "Blast, blast, blast!" she said, pressing on. "Why do I have to be this way?"

"Ebba! Ebba, what's wrong?" Daniel asked as he ran toward her.

Ebba sneezed and looked at him, or tried to. "I'm fine, I just..." She sneezed again, and started to cry.

"Ah, sweetie, ya poor thing. Ya must be plumb miserable. Do ya know what's wrong?"

"Of course I know what's wrong!" she yelped, then sneezed again. "It's just that I don't know what to do about it!" More sneezing.

Daniel swallowed hard, trying to figure out what to do, then reached into his pocket, pulled out a handkerchief and handed it to her. "Here, take this."

She grabbed at empty air, unable to see it, until he put it in her hand. She immediately blew her nose with it, then promptly sneezed some more.

"Great jumpin' horny toads!" Daniel exclaimed. "I ain't never seen nothin' like this!"

"You're not helping," she groaned, and blew her nose again.

Daniel, unsure of what else to do, began to chuckle. "I'm sorry, sweetie, it's just that I ain't never seen someone sneeze so much."

"Well, I have, just about every day of my life!"

Daniel laughed. "I still don't believe it."

"You have eyes, don't you?" She pointed at herself, sniffled, and sneezed again.

"Ain't there no way to make it stop?" he asked helplessly.

"If there was, do you think I'd be standing here like this?!" she asked tersely.

"No need to bite my head off. I was just askin'."

"Your mother…*achoo! achoo!*…gave me something yesterday…*sniff*…it seemed to help."

Daniel nodded, pulled her against him, then picked her up.

"What are you doing?" she screeched.

"Gettin' ya back to the house as fast as I can 'fore ya plumb sneeze yerself to death!"

"I'm not going to sneeze myself to death!" The only reason she knew that was that if it were possible, she'd have been dead a long time ago. "Put me down!"

"Nope," he said firmly. "Yer eyes are so full of tears ya can't see straight anyways. Yer liable to walk right into a tree and knock yerself out."

She couldn't even answer—the sneezes were coming thick and fast now.

"Land sakes, darlin', don't die on me! We ain't even married yet!"

"No one is…*achoo!*…dying!" she whined. Though the thought did have merit—at least she wouldn't be sneezing anymore.

Daniel picked up the pace. "Don't ya worry none, sweetie. As soon as we get back to the house I'll have Ma fix ya up. She can fix anythin'."

"I'm glad you hab such codfidence id your mother's abilities," she said, her nose so stuffed now she could barely breathe, let alone talk.

"She helped ya yesterday, didn't she?" he asked as they reached the barnyard.

"Yes," she croaked. Great. There went her voice again.

Just then Ma ran out the back door and headed straight for them. "Good Lord, what happened? Did she fall and break her leg?"

Achoo! Achoo! Achoo!

"Oh," Ma said. "That again, is it?"

Ebba watched Ma study her through bleary eyes. "I thigk it's the orchards," she suggested.

"Bring her inside, Daniel," Ma instructed. "Plop her down in the kitchen and I'll take care of the rest. Then you can get back to work."

"Sure thing, Ma." He headed up the back steps, carried Ebba through the open kitchen door and straight to the table where he set her on her feet next to it. "Ma'll set ya straight, ya'll see." Then to her surprise, he tenderly brushed the hair out of her eyes and wiped at the tears around them. "I feel powerful sorry for ya right now, darlin'. I wish there was somethin' else I could do."

Ebba could only shake her head, not sure if her voice would even work. She tried to smile, but sneezed instead.

His eyes filled with determination, and he pulled her into his arms for a hug. "I gotta get back to work, sweetie. But I know that by the time I see ya again ya'll be right as rain." He kissed her hair, and between that and her stuffy nose, it was all she could do to remain standing.

Chapter Nine

Daniel stomped back to work. Maybe if he picked up his pace, the tight feeling in his chest would lessen and he'd be able to breathe better. Fear had a way of sucking the wind out of him, and he wasn't as accustomed to fighting it as his brothers were. They were experienced in protecting their women from harm. But how was he going to protect his from this? It was one thing to battle an outlaw, or some bungling intruder that managed to get into the house, or even a jealous rival. But sickness and disease were another thing altogether.

Maybe he was just overreacting. But it didn't feel like it.

Ebba was sneezing something awful and could hardly see for the tears in her eyes. Had she been crying because she was in pain? Was her ailment really that bad? Or did she just not do well around apple trees? He knew Warren Johnson would start to sneeze come springtime—it would last for a few weeks, then clear up and go away. Was that what Ebba suffered? But her sneezing was much worse than Warren's.

He certainly hoped Ma could fix her. He didn't like the idea of Ebba sneezing her way through their wedding vows.

"What was the ruckus up at the house?" Benjamin asked as he brought their plow horse Myrtle to a stop and wiped his brow.

"Poor Ebba," Daniel said with a shake of his head. "She ain't feelin' well right now. I hate to say this, Benjamin, but I don't think the trees here are good for her."

"The trees?" Benjamin said in surprise. "What do trees have to do with anythin'?"

"Everythin', if I figger right. She sneezes like Warren Johnson does when the orchards start in to blossomin'."

"Oh, that," Benjamin said with a wave of his hand. "That ain't nothin' To worry 'bout. Ma can give her something that'll help. I'd be more worried about the weddin' if I were ya."

"Yeah, I suppose yer right. But I cain't help but worry 'bout her. Ya shoulda seen her! She sneezed and sneezed and sneezed and couldn't stop. Land sakes, I thought she was gonna sneeze her whole head off."

Benjamin started to chuckle, then stopped. "I know it ain't funny, poor thing, but I cain't help but picture that in my head."

"Fine, go ahead and laugh. You're not the one's gonna be marryin' her in a couple days."

"Don't go takin' offense, little brother. I was just kiddin' with ya."

"It ain't funny. What if she's powerful sick or somethin'?"

"Don't get sore—I told ya I didn't mean nothin' by it. Besides, she'll be fine. Ya plumb worry like a mother hen."

Daniel patted Myrtle's neck and scratched her between the ears. "It ain't just her sneezin'."

"What do ya mean?" Benjamin asked.

"Folks in town were lookin' at her funny-like. I didn't pay too much attention to it 'til she asked if they were the unfriendly type."

"Folks in Nowhere?" Benjamin said, a little shocked. "That *is* odd."

"I thought she was just bein', ya know, oversensitive, her bein' new in town and all. But then I got to lookin' around when I walked her back to the hotel, and by golly if they weren't looking at her funny. Like they didn't want her there at all."

"Strange." Benjamin scratched his head. "Did Ma notice?"

"If'n she did, she's not sayin' nothin'. She won't want to upset Ebba."

"Yer right," Benjamin agreed. "Well, yer not in town now, are ya?"

"No, but the town's comin' here soon. What if folks look at her all strange durin' our weddin'? How's that gonna make Ebba feel?"

"Personally, I wouldn't worry about it 'til the time comes. I wager folks'll wanna talk to Ebba and get to know her. 'Fore the day's out, half of 'em will've invited the two of ya to Sunday supper. Best get them funny thoughts out of yer head."

"Oh, all right." Daniel gave Myrtle one last pat on the neck. "Ya want me to take over for a while?"

"Thanks, I appreciate it. I'd like to get up to the house and check on Sebastian. He's been sneezin' too."

"Guess it's just in the air." Daniel positioned himself behind the plow, unwrapped the lines and, with a whistle and a slap, got Myrtle moving.

"Is this the same thing you gave me back in town?" Ebba asked.

"No, this is a little different," Ma said. "On account of I don't keep alcohol in this house."

"Alcohol?" Ebba said in shock. "You mean that concoction I drank the other night was…was…"

"One of the ingredients was whiskey," Ma explained. "I bet you slept like a baby too."

"You gave me whiskey?" Ebba said between coughs.

"Only because they didn't have any brandy. That works best for a scratchy throat."

"Dear me. What else was in that stuff you made me drink?"

"I didn't make you drink it. I offered it to you and you drank it yourself."

"That's because you didn't tell me what it was. If I had known there was whiskey in it, I probably wouldn't have drunk it at all."

"And go on suffering with all that sneezing? Somehow I think you'd have drunk it down anyway, child.

But we can argue about that another time. It worked, didn't it?"

"Yes," Ebba said with a sigh. "It did."

"Well, I'm glad we agree on that. The problem now is trying to make something that will work as well without the liquor in it." Ma sat at the kitchen table and began drumming her fingers on the surface. "We could try some apple cider…"

"Apple cider?"

"Yes, it works wonders." Ma clasped her hands in front of her on the table. "At least, it'll make you feel better. Not sure what it'll do for your sneezing."

Ebba wiped her nose with a handkerchief. "I'll try anything, especially if it doesn't involve alcohol. Do you realize that's the first alcohol I've ever had in my life?"

"I'm not sure it counts, being as how it was medicinal," Ma said with a grin.

Ebba closed her eyes and shook her head as if she just lost a horrible battle.

"Now don't go giving me that sort of look," said Ma. "Folks around here have a little nip when they're cold or not feeling well. Besides, in the Good Book Saint Paul told Timothy to have a little wine for his ailments, and Saint Paul was smarter than you or me, I figure. It's not like we're all down at the saloon guzzling the stuff!"

Ebba opened her eyes and looked at her. "I know you didn't mean it that way. It's just that I… I've seen what liquor can do to a man, not to mention a woman."

Ma's grin vanished. "What are you talking about, child?"

Ebba, who'd been standing near the table all this time, sat. "We had neighbors when we lived in Chicago for a short time, a husband and wife. They drank every night, then fought like two devils trying to kill each other. The drunker they got, the worse they fought. I think that's one of the reasons we moved to Denver, that and my parents' health."

"Why, that's terrible!" Ma said. "No wonder you don't want to have anything to do with whiskey. But don't you worry none, child. None of my boys touch it, except as medicine."

Ebba smiled. "That's good to know." The teakettle began to whistle, and she got up, took a hot pad and plucked it off the stove. She went to the teapot and began to fill it with the hot water.

"Oh, Ebba," Ma said.

Ebba stopped pouring and looked at her. "Yes?"

"Have you noticed you haven't sneezed since you've been in the house?"

Ebba glanced between the teakettle and Ma. "By Heaven, you're right, I haven't. I wonder why that is?"

"I think some of it might have to do with my heating water in here for dishes earlier. Takes some of the dryness out of the air. The teakettle does the same. It helps your nose."

Ebba put the lid on the teapot to let it steep then returned the kettle to the stove. "Maybe I should let the water boil some more."

"Couldn't hurt to try. You know, when my boys

were young and would get to coughing come winter-time, I noticed water boiling on the stove seemed to help them. They wouldn't cough as much when they were here in the kitchen."

"Isn't it amazing how the air affects us?" Ebba said. Perhaps it was a silly thing to say, but she did notice the difference.

"Are you excited about your wedding?" Ma asked, changing the subject.

"I'm getting there. I just don't want to make a fool of myself once Daniel and I are standing in front of the preacher. I'd hate to start sneezing."

"I'll see what I can do about fixing you something to help. Maybe what we're doing now, you can do before you say your vows. Have yourself a nice cup of tea, then put some water on the stove and get some steam in the air."

"Won't that be hard to do with a house full of people?"

"It's your wedding, child," Ma replied. "You do what you want."

After Ebba and Ma finished their tea, they went into the sewing room. "There now," Ma said. "Doesn't that look nice?"

Ebba studied her wedding dress hanging on the back of the door. "It looks prettier now than when Mrs. Pettigrew gave it to me," she said.

"I'll take that as a compliment. But it was nothing an iron couldn't handle."

"You did a wonderful job, Ma. Thank you."

"It was nothing. You'd have done the same for me."

Ebba sighed as she admired her gown. She hadn't

even tried it on yet—there hadn't been time before she left Denver. "I hope it fits."

"What do you mean, you hope it fits?"

"Mrs. Pettigrew guessed at my size."

"Then don't just stand there gawking at it, child. Let's try it on." Ma took the dress off its hanger and shook it out a little. "I'm sure it'll fit—I don't see why it wouldn't. But something like this should never be left to chance, child. If it needs to be taken in or out, I'll be able to get it done overnight."

"Oh no, I couldn't let you do that. It's my dress, so my responsibility."

"If that were the case, then *you* should have ironed it," Ma said with a wink.

Ebba looked away a moment. "You're right. I should've been the one to do the work. I'm sorry."

"Don't apologize for it, child. I didn't mind doing the ironing. It's a beautiful dress—it was a privilege."

Ebba thought about that for a moment and came to a realization. "Sewing is a passion for you, isn't it?

"It certainly is," Ma said with a dreamy look. "I've sewn since I was a little girl, anything I could get my hands on. I liked to experiment."

Ebba looked around the room and noticed the elaborate display of ribbons, threads, fabric, feathers, jars of buttons and other sewing paraphernalia. "This must be your haven."

"It is. Every woman needs one. Bella, she goes down and sits on a log by the creek."

Ebba smiled. "She does?"

"Oh yes. And Charity likes to take a book and go

read in the hayloft. I play with Sebastian and Truly while she has a break."

"And what about Samijo? What does she do?"

"Her haven is her children. That and baking." Ma handed the dress to Ebba. "All right, put it on and let's see what we're looking at."

Ebba stepped behind a dressing screen, took off her dress and put the other one on. Soon she had everything where it was supposed to be and stepped out for inspection. "Well, what do you think?"

Ma walked around her and played with the skirt here and there. "Hmmm...let's button you up to be sure, but I think Mrs. Pettigrew guessed right."

Ebba smiled and breathed a sigh of relief. The last thing she wanted was for Ma to be up half the night taking in her wedding dress. By the same token, she didn't want to be up half the night doing it either.

Ma did up the buttons and walked a circle a second time. "My my, will you look at that. It's beautiful, Ebba, simply beautiful."

Ebba spied a full-length mirror, went to stand before it and gasped when she saw her reflection. "I've never seen myself like this before. I look like a princess."

"Daniel is going to bust a gut when he sees you," Ma said.

"As long as he doesn't bust anything else," Ebba said with a laugh.

"Let's hope not," Ma said. "Then again, maybe the sight of you will keep him from being so nervous. Calvin and Benjamin were beside themselves when they got married."

"I'm sure I'll be nervous too," Ebba admitted.

"All brides are nervous on their wedding day. But don't you worry none—you and Daniel will be good together. I can tell already."

Ebba turned to face her. "How can you tell? Daniel and I don't even know each other yet. We're each marrying a perfect stranger."

"So did Arlan, Benjamin and Calvin. All three of my boys got mail-order brides. Now Daniel makes four."

"But how did they manage it? Are they all in love?"

"Of course they are," Ma said. "They're all happily married men thanks to one thing."

"Only one?" asked Ebba. "I thought it took a good many things to make a marriage work."

"True enough, child. But this is a philosophy I learned with my own husband when he was alive. We passed it on to our children when they were young to make sure they stood by it when they were old enough to marry."

"What is it?" Ebba had forgotten about her beautiful dress now, her eyes intense on Ma.

"That you have three things in your pocket before you get married, or at least be mindful of them as they grow during the marriage. Sometimes it takes time to get all three, and that's okay. But to make a marriage really work, you need them all."

"Don't keep me in suspense—what are they?"

"All right, I'll tell you." Ma held up a finger. "Number one, you have to like your husband."

Ebba blinked a few times. "I have that in my pocket

already. I like Daniel. From what I know of him, I think he's sweet, kind and he looks out for you. He carried me across the orchard just because I was sneezing."

"Yes, he sure enough did," Ma said with a laugh, then held up another finger. "Number two, you have to love him."

"It's too early for that, I'm afraid," Ebba said with a hint of disappointment. She'd only known the man for a few days; there was no way she could love him yet.

"You'll come to love Daniel in time, just as he'll come to love you," Ma said. "I'm sure of it. Which brings me to number three." She held up the last finger.

"What?"

"You have to be *in* love with him."

Ebba stared at her. "I don't understand. What's the difference between loving Daniel and being in love with him?"

"Exactly," Ma said with a grin. "Most folks don't understand that there's a difference."

"What is it?"

"That, child, you're going to have to find out for yourself. Everyone's different, and what their love looks like for another person is different. But trust me—you'll know when you get there."

Chapter Ten

The rest of the day was spent cleaning house, baking cookies, organizing sleeping arrangements for the wedding guests and (for Ebba, anyway) learning everyone's names. "Now let me see…" She eyed the Italian boy staring back at her. "You're Arturo, right?"

"That's right!" he said with a smile. "Now the rest!"

Ebba studied the two girls standing next to him. Arturo, she knew, was ten and a half. One of the girls wasn't much younger, the other younger still. "This is going to be harder," she admitted, then bit her lip in concentration. "Don't tell me. Just give me a minute."

The two girls started to giggle, but quickly slapped their hands over their mouths to stifle it. "What do we get if she guesses wrong?" one of them asked their older brother.

"I don't know." He shrugged and looked at Ebba. "What do they get?"

She held out her empty hands. "I have nothing to give you, I'm afraid."

The younger girl stomped her foot. "Then I'm not going to tell you my name."

The other girl rolled her eyes. "Her name is Gabriella, but we call her Gabby."

"That's not fair!" Gabby cried. "Fine then! *Her* name is Melania, but we call her *Mel*."

"Is that so?" Ebba said with a nod. "All right then, we have Arturo, Gabby and Mel."

"I'm six!" Gabby blurted.

"You are?" Ebba said enthusiastically. "You're very tall for six." In fact, all of Bella's brothers and sisters seemed tall for their age. Arturo might be ten and a half, but was almost as tall as his twelve-year-old sister, Lucia. "How old are you, Mel?"

"I'm nine," she said proudly.

"So let me see if I have this," Ebba said. "Rufina's the oldest, right?"

"She's sixteen," Arturo volunteered.

"Right," Ebba said. "Then there's Alfonso and he's fifteen?"

"Fourteen," Gabby corrected with a grin.

"Fourteen," Ebba repeated. She tapped at her temple as if that would help her remember. "Lucia is twelve. Arturo; you're ten and a half, Mel is nine, Leo… Leonardo…"

"We just call him Leo," Mel said. "And he's seven and a half, remember?"

"I do now, but after an hour I probably won't," Ebba admitted.

"And that doesn't even include our other brothers!" Gabby added, hopping up and down.

"Good heavens, there are more of you?" Ebba squeaked.

"Of course there is," Arturo said as if offended. "Don't you remember them from this morning?"

"I'm afraid this day has me a little muddled, children, what with the wedding and all. You'll excuse me if I have to ask you to remind me about things?"

"That's okay," Mel said. "We forget things too."

"What are your brother's names?" Ebba asked with a smile. Not that she'd remember them by the time the children left to go home.

"Thatcher is two," Arturo said. "And the twins, Alastair and Hugh, are six months old."

Ebba sighed. "There's no shortage of twins in this family, is there?"

"I bet you and Daniel will have twins," Arturo said. "*Zio* Calvin said so."

Ebba walked over to the kitchen table and sat. "How about letting Daniel and I get married first, then we'll see what happens?" she said diplomatically.

"I bet you have *triplets*!" Gabby said and started bouncing again.

"Oh dear me," Ebba said in a rush. "That's too much to think about at the moment. Let me concentrate on my wedding for now."

The children laughed. "You're fun to talk to—I wish we could stay longer," Arturo said. He put his hands on the shoulders of his sisters. "Let's go find Bella. I know she has work for us to do."

"Can we call you *Zia* Ebba?" Gabby asked.

Zia must mean "aunt," Ebba realized. "Of course

you can. Once I marry Daniel, that's exactly what I'll become."

"Hooray!" Gabby said and started to jump again.

Arturo gave her a gentle shove and guided her and Mel to the kitchen's backdoor. "My sister Bella will want you to come to dinner. You will tonight, won't you?"

Ebba gave him a blank look. She could hardly think straight, let alone plan where she would eat later that day. "I'll have to leave that up to Daniel, I'm afraid. For all I know I might be cooking supper here."

"You won't have to cook supper yet—you're getting married," Mel chimed. "Once you are, *then* you'll have to do all the work."

Ebba smiled nervously. "Well, I suppose that's good to know." She wasn't sure if the child was joking or not.

Arturo grinned and, with Mel and Gabby in tow, left the house.

Okay, definitely joking. Ebba sighed in relief and closed her eyes a moment. The day had been a whirlwind, and she felt like a tumbleweed tossed around by it. She hadn't expected there to be so many people, all of which she was about to be related to. "Auntie Ebba," she mused aloud. By her estimation, she was about to inherit six brothers and sisters-in-law and... fifteen nieces and nephews?

"Oh my Lord," she whispered as the realization hit. "It's like a small town out here." In which she was the only newcomer—and everyone had the same surname...

She pushed the thought aside, got up from the table and poured herself a cup of coffee. It was near three-thirty and Charity would be starting supper soon. She wanted to help, but wasn't sure what Charity would have her do. Then she heard footsteps descending the stairs and figured she'd soon find out.

But it was Rufina, not Charity, who entered the kitchen. *Sixteen, oldest of Bella's siblings, everyone calls her Rufi,* Ebba quickly reviewed in her mind.

"Hello," the girl greeted her.

"Good afternoon," Ebba said. "Is Charity upstairs?"

"Yes, she's feeding Truly. She asked me to come down and get things started."

"For supper?" Ebba asked. "If so, I'd like to help."

"Yes, *grazie*." The girl went to the stove, grabbed a couple of pieces from the wood box in the corner and stuffed them into the stove's firebox. That done, she started gathering what they'd need to prepare supper: pots, pans, and a mixing bowl.

"How can I help you?" Ebba asked. She'd never seen anyone work so fast.

"We're going to make chicken and dumplings," Rufi announced. "There are potatoes in the root cellar outside. Why don't you fetch a basketful?"

Ebba glanced around. "Where's the basket?"

"In the root cellar, silly. After you fetch the potatoes, then you return it."

Ebba nodded and left the kitchen. Samijo had pointed out the root cellar when they'd gone to her house earlier that morning. Once there, she found several baskets, took one and hoped the potatoes weren't in some dark corner. She wasn't fond of reaching into such places, especially if something with more than two legs had set up house there. The cellar was large and the only light was from the open door.

Thankfully, she spotted the potatoes and easily got the job done. She went back to the house, took the potatoes out of the basket, and was headed to the root cellar to return it when the sneezing started. "Oh no, not again!"

She hurried back to the house as fast as she could, grabbed the kettle, then ran outside to the pump to fill it. Returning to the kitchen, she set it on the stove and breathed a sigh of relief.

Rufi gave her a confused look. "Are you in a hurry to make some tea?"

"It helps with…with…" She sneezed again. "…with that."

"Didn't *Nonna* make you chamomile tea? That's what helps me."

"Chamomile tea?" Ebba said in surprise. "I'm not sure. We had tea earlier today, but I didn't know what kind it was."

"Did it help with the sneezing?" Rufi asked.

Ebba made to sneeze again but held a finger under her nose to stop it. "Yes, it did!"

"Well then, don't just stand there, make yourself a cup," Rufi said with a laugh.

Ebba went to do just that before she fell into a full sneezing fit. For Heaven's sake, around here all she had to do was go outside to get one going. At least in the city it took a while. But here in the Weavers' little valley, such was not the case. And if she was going to live here, she'd have to figure out what to do. "How much tea does Ma have in the house?" she mused aloud.

"I have no idea, but with all your sneezing she won't have it for long." Rufi seemed far too amused by her suffering.

"Oh my heavens," Ebba said, alarmed. "That means we'll have to make another trip to town to get more. What an endeavor that will be!" Endeavor, indeed. Would Daniel make the trip just because she was sneezing her head off? Would she even be up to going with him? This ailment of hers was more trouble than it was worth. Could a man divorce a woman on grounds of allergies?

"I hear ginger tea works well too. At least that's what my *nonna* in New York told me," said Rufi.

Ebba already had a cup and saucer out. She grabbed the tea canister she'd seen Ma use earlier and opened it—half-full! "Oh good, there's enough." But how long would it take her to use it all up?

"I'll get the chicken ready," Rufi told her. "After you have your tea you can peel the potatoes. Is that all right?"

Ebba nodded, a finger still under her nose as she did her best not to start sneezing again. Soon the kettle began to boil and with a sigh of relief she fixed herself a cup of tea. That done, she found a knife she could use to peel the potatoes and got to work.

"Aren't you going to drink your tea first?" Rufi asked.

"I'll drink it as I peel. Don't worry, I'll try not to sneeze on the potatoes."

It was meant as a joke, but Rufi grimaced anyway before returning to her own work. Neither of them talked for a while until Rufi broke the silence. "Are you excited to get married?"

Ebba stopped peeling. "I will be if I can stop sneezing long enough."

"You must be miserable." Rufi continued to work.

"Not all the time," Ebba said. "But out here is definitely…difficult. I can't imagine feeling like this day in and day out."

Rufi turned to face her. "I'm sorry that you suffer. I get like that sometimes, but nothing like you. I hope one day when I am married that I don't…" She snapped her mouth shut and covered it with a hand, then just as quickly removed it. "I'm sorry, I did not mean to make it sound like…"

"Like the end of the world?" Ebba asked.

"I did not mean it that way."

Ebba sighed and nodded. "I understand." She looked the girl over. As all the other Weavers said, she really was beautiful and would have no problem finding herself a husband when she was old enough. But even as pretty as she was, what if Rufi suffered the same thing Ebba did? She laughed at the thought.

"What's so funny?"

Ebba waved a hand at her, then pointed to her nose. "This. How long do you think Daniel will last before he decides he doesn't want a sneezing wife?"

Rufi looked shocked. "Don't say such a thing! Daniel and his brothers are good men! They would never think of backing out of a marriage because of a silly thing as sneezing!"

Ebba stared at her moment. She noticed her Italian accent got thicker when she was angry. And the girl was angry—her stance had become defiant, feet apart, hands balled into fists. "I'm sorry if that offended you. I didn't mean to insult the Weaver men, especially not when I'm about to marry one. It's just that I feel so helpless when I get like this."

"You're not sneezing now," Rufi pointed out. "It seems to have stopped."

Ebba took another sip of tea. "That's because I'm not outside. It gets better when I'm in the house. The tea helps too."

Rufi went to the table and sat. "Don't worry, Ebba. We'll figure out what helps and what doesn't. Besides, come harvest time we all have to work outside. You can't stay in the house forever."

"No," Ebba said in dismay. "I can't."

Ebba spent the rest of the evening in despair, and not even Daniel's happy countenance was enough to pull her out of the pit. He smiled at her from across the kitchen table at suppertime, made jokes with Benjamin and chuckled every time Sebastian tossed the spoon off his high chair.

But nothing seemed to help. All Ebba could think about was a life spent locked indoors for her health's sake. Rufi was right—she couldn't just hide inside the farmhouse. She'd have to go outside at some point. And what about summer? The days would be growing hotter, and that meant open windows. What was she going to do then? She couldn't expect everyone else to suffer the summer heat because of her.

She knew marrying a farmer wasn't a good idea. She should've waited for another prospect to come along. So what if it meant months and months of extra work and verbal abuse from Mrs. Feldnick? Maybe she could have found a husband that lived by the seashore. Or maybe Oregon—she'd heard parts of Oregon were nice and rainy…

"What's the matter, sweetie?"

Ebba looked at Daniel across the table, her eyes itchy and red. The sneezing had stopped, but her eyes hadn't. "Nothing," she said.

"I don't believe ya."

She didn't feel like debating. "It's nothing, really."

"Seems a shame to waste a nice evening like this," Ma said. "Why don't the two of you go sit on the front porch for a while and get better acquainted?"

Ebba's eyes widened in horror. "Ma, I can't…"

Ma's own eyes narrowed in determination. "You can and you will. I'll put the kettle on."

"But Ma, you know what will happen the moment I step outside…"

"I do. How else will we figure out how to help you if we don't have something to fix? I'm going to try a different remedy—and to do that I need you sneezing."

Ebba's entire face twisted up in consternation. "You must be joking." Was she about to become a science experiment?!

Apparently, yes, she was. "I most certainly am not

joking," Ma replied. "Daniel, take your bride out to the front porch and do some sparking or something."

Daniel's eyes lit up. "Yes, ma'am!" He sprang up from his chair and came around the table to where Ebba sat. "Ya heard the woman—let's go!"

"Are you out of your mind?" Ebba gasped, gripping the table with both hands. "This will never work."

"How will you know unless you try?" Ma asked.

Ebba shook her head. "I can't subject Daniel to this, let alone all of you."

"Oh, stop fussing, get on out there and kiss the man!" Ma insisted.

Ebba's eyes went round as platters. "Mrs. Weaver!"

"Ma, if you please. Now get!"

"Best do as she says, sweetie. Otherwise, she'll bust a gut—and then bust one of us." Daniel took her by the arm, pulled her to her feet, took her hand and headed for the hall.

"Let go of me," Ebba said, trying to pull away.

"Stop it, Ebba. You heard Ma—let's go outside and see what happens."

"I know exactly what's going to happen. The same thing that happened when you found me in the orchard."

By now they were at the front door. "So?"

She stared at him in shock. "Do you really want to put up with *that* the rest of your life?"

"The rest of my life?" he said as he opened the door. He gave her a gentle tug and pulled her onto the front porch. "What sort of talk is that?"

Ebba tried to pull her hand out of his and failed. "Please, let me go back inside…"

But Daniel took her other hand with his free one and pulled her flush against him. His arms snaked around her, making her his prisoner. "Don't ya know it's like Ma said? She cain't tell if somethin's workin' if'n yer not sneezin'."

He led her to a porch swing and sat them both down, never once letting her go. "Now I'm sorry ya suffer so, sweetie, but yer gonna be my wife. That means for richer or poorer, in sickness and in health and all that other stuff the preacher's gonna say to us come our weddin' day." He pulled away enough to look at her. "We got one more day 'til we get hitched, Ebba. Ya need to stop thinkin' ya can't marry me just 'cause ya got a runny nose. That's kinda ridiculous, if ya don't mind me sayin'."

Ebba blushed. "It's just that…oh, I know it's silly, but then again, it's not. What if Ma can't fix it?"

"She fixed it once already, didn't she?"

"Yes, but that was only because she used…well… whiskey."

"Whiskey?" Daniel said in surprise. "So that's why ya couldn't remember where ya were the next mornin'!"

"*That* is not the reason!"

"Ain't it?" he teased. "I bet ya slept real good that night too."

"Ohhhh, why am I even trying to explain this to you?" she asked in exasperation. "You're not listening to me!"

"Sure I am, darlin'. Yer afraid all this sneezin' and coughin' is gonna be a bother to me once we're married, is that right?"

Ebba stared at him in shock. "Yes," she said, her voice barely above a whisper. "I am."

"Well, I'll tell ya right now, I ain't worried 'bout it. I know sure as the sun sets that Ma'll figure somethin' out for ya. She always does."

Ebba sighed heavily…and felt her nose start to tickle. *Here it comes…*

"Look at me, sweetie," Daniel instructed.

Ebba looked into his eyes, gasped at the tenderness in them…and sneezed. All over him.

After a second of stunned silence, he laughed, took out his handkerchief and wiped his face. Then he pulled her close. "Ya know what?" he asked gently.

She sneezed again, though thankfully she had time to turn her head first. "What?" she asked miserably.

"I think we're gonna get along just fine."

She pushed them apart to look at him. "What makes you say that?"

"Shucks, darlin', if'n I can survive being tossed down a well half my life by my brothers, then I can survive a little sneezin'."

She blinked. "Tossed down a well?!"

Daniel laughed again, pulled her close and kissed the top of her head. "Yep, I figger I can survive just about anythin'. I'll survive ya too."

Chapter Eleven

The next day the guests began to arrive, and Ebba grew more nervous by the minute. As predicted, stepping out (well, forced out) onto the front porch with Daniel had sent her into a sneezing fit within minutes. But another dose of chamomile tea, this time with a bit of honey added, helped calm her throat before it got out of hand.

Come bedtime Ebba finally conceded. Ma was right—they would just have to experiment and find out what worked and what didn't. "Fine, you win," she'd told Daniel as he'd led her upstairs to her room.

"It's like I told ya, sweetie—ya just hafta trust Ma knows what she's doing. I knew she'd help. She'll do whatever it takes to find what works for ya."

"I guess I owe you an apology," Ebba said, her eyes downcast.

Daniel tucked a finger under her chin and lifted her face to his. "Ain't nothin' To be ashamed of, Ebba. You need to learn to give folks a chance, is all."

"If you say so, Daniel. I'll try to be better about that in the future."

"I'm sure ya will." He leaned down and kissed her on the forehead again. "G'night, sweetie. I'll see ya in the mornin'." He turned on his heel and disappeared down the stairs. And Ebba had dreamt about that gentle kiss all night.

But today was a new day—not to mention the day before her wedding—and there was a lot of work to be done.

"Mary," Leona Riley called out. "Did you think about a veil for the bride?"

"Land sakes, no!" Ma called as she came out of the sewing room. "I was so concerned about getting the dress ready, I forgot all about a veil."

"Then it's a good thing I thought of it." Leona pulled a veil out of a box. "Let's see how this looks on her."

"I'm just glad I had one in the store," added Aunt Betsy. "Of course, it's not like my sister to not have what she needs to make one, but there isn't time."

"For once, sister dear, I agree with you." Ma turned toward the hall. "Ebba!"

Ebba came out of the kitchen and into the parlor, her hands and apron spotted with flour. "What is it, Ma?"

"For Heaven's sake, child, stop fussing in the kitchen!" Ma chastised. "We need to get you ready for your wedding."

"The wedding isn't until tomorrow, Ma," Ebba protested, then saw the veil in Mrs. Riley's hands. "What's that?"

"Something beautiful for a beautiful bride," Aunt

Betsy explained. "I can't wait to see you in your wedding dress."

"Yes, let's have a look," Leona said. "Then we can see how the veil goes with it."

Ebba glanced at the three matrons, all with eager looks on their faces. "Shouldn't I finish the biscuits first?"

"Is Rufi in the kitchen with you?" Ma asked.

"Yes, she is."

"Then she can take over the biscuits. She knows you have to get ready for tomorrow."

Ebba fought against a sigh. It wasn't even noon and she was already exhausted. The thought of trying on her wedding dress who knew how many times made her want to hide in the barn. "Very well. I'll let Rufi know."

"I'll let her know." Leona marched toward the kitchen. "You put on that dress."

Aunt Betsy clapped her hands together in glee. "I do love a good wedding!" She hurried toward the sewing room.

Ma watched her go and rolled her eyes. "I hope they don't get too frenzied over this."

"Frenzied?" Ebba asked, worried.

"I'm afraid so, child. You see, Leona and your Aunt Betsy can get *very* excited when it comes to weddings. In fact, if there aren't any weddings going on, they tend to make them happen."

Ebba swallowed hard and took a step back, then glanced toward the kitchen, thinking of poor Rufi. The girl was probably next on their list. Thankfully, she was still too young to marry, but not for long…

"Well, let's get this over with," said Ma. "I have to admit, I am curious how that veil will look. Maybe we can spruce it up if you don't like it."

It didn't take long before Ebba was into her wedding dress and the three matrons went to work. Aunt Betsy played with her hair while Ma and Leona discussed the veil. When they finally put it on her head, Ma looked very pleased. "It's beautiful," she said.

And Ebba had to agree—she looked better today than she had the day before. The veil definitely completed the look. Now she would truly be a bride—or at least feel like one. She could hardly believe she was to be married in less than twenty-four hours.

Speaking of which… "When will the other guests arrive?"

"Mr. and Mrs. Davis will be here tonight along with Matthew and Charlotte," Aunt Betsy volunteered. "It's too bad Billy and Abbey aren't going to make it."

"Who are Billy and Abbey?" Ebba asked.

"Charlotte's younger sister and her husband," Leona explained. "They moved to Clear Creek, Oregon—you know, the town my brother is from?"

"Oh yes, where is the sheriff?" Ebba glanced at Ma to see her reaction.

"He's riding out with Tom and Rose Turner," Leona said. "He's been wanting to talk with Tom the entire time he's been here. I can't understand why."

Ebba watched Ma's cheeks grow pink and smiled. Daniel was right—Ma *was* sweet on the sheriff. "Well, they are both lawmen and from the same hometown.

Why wouldn't he want to spend time with Deputy Turner?"

"Of course he would," Ma said. She turned to Leona. "Will your brother be going home with you the day after the wedding?"

"I assume so, but Harlan does what he wants," Leona said.

Ma's eyes darted around the room as she licked her lips. "Men often do."

"Do you like your hair this way, Ebba?" Aunt Betsy asked.

"It's very fine. Thank you for styling it for me. Do you think Daniel will like it?"

"He'll love it, child," Ma said with a smile. "He'll love you."

Ebba caught the tremor in her voice. Daniel was her baby, the last of her children to marry. She hadn't thought about how her new mother-in-law would feel, other than ecstatically happy. Sadness had never occurred to her. "Are you referring to what we talked about the other day? That kind of love?"

Ma smiled and took her hands in her own. "It'll be a good start, child. A very good start."

"Stop it, I tell ya!" Daniel shouted over his brothers' boisterous laughter. The twins each had one of his ankles in their grasp as they held him headfirst over the well. Thankfully it was deep, wide and full of water. Daniel knew to tuck himself into a ball the minute they let go. After all, this was hardly the first time they'd done this—and possibly not the last.

"C'mon, Daniel," Calvin said with a snicker. "It's yer last day as a free man—and *our* last time to throw ya in the well as one!"

Daniel's arms splayed helplessly as he struggled. "Dagnabit, I got chores to do! Ma's gonna have a fit when she finds out we ain't got 'em done in time!"

"Well, what do we have here?" a man's voice drawled above him. Daniel tried to see who it was but couldn't quite manage it.

"Howdy, Deputy!" Calvin replied happily. "Yer just in time!"

"Ya sure are," said Benjamin. "This here's what ya might call a monumental occasion."

"Daniel?" the voice called down the well, "is that you?"

"Yes, it's me! Who else would these idjit brothers of mine be hangin' on to like this?"

"Seems to me it's a good thing they are, or ya'd be splashin' around down there by now."

"They're a bad influence on the younguns!" Daniel called back. He shook his head. His brothers usually didn't hold him upside down for this long—they'd just get him in position and let go. Now that they had an audience, who knew what they'd do? "Just get it over with, why don't ya!"

"Ya should've seen how hard he fought us, Deputy Turner," Calvin said with pride. "Almost got away from us twice."

"And I woulda if Alfonso hadn't tripped me!" Daniel groused.

"That's right," Benjamin chortled from above. "Remind me to give that boy a penny, will ya, Calvin?"

"Sure will, brother," Calvin chuckled.

"Ain't you boys gettin' kinda tired of holdin' yer brother like that?" Deputy Turner asked.

"Yeah, come to think of it," Calvin said, his voice starting to strain. "What do ya think, Benjamin? Should we drop him?"

Benjamin shrugged. "On the count of three?"

"Okay. Deputy, ya wanna count?" Calvin asked.

"I'd better not," he said. "In my position, I cain't be seen to condone unlawful behavior."

Daniel could just imagine the grin on his face. "Oh for crying out loud, just do it already! I got chores to finish!"

"Yer awful anxious to get wet," the deputy pointed out. "But I suppose these boys can't hold ya like this forever."

"One…two…"

Benjamin was interrupted by another voice. "What's going on here?"

"Oh, for the love of Pete," Daniel grumbled. He was starting to get dizzy from being upside down for so long. If they didn't let go of him soon, he might have trouble when he hit the water "Just do it!"

"Great Scott! Is that Daniel you two have a hold of?" Daniel recognized the voice of Sheriff Hughes.

"Harlan, if'n they don't let go, arrest 'em! I'm startin' to feel kinda poorly down here."

"You heard him, boys," the sheriff agreed.

"Three," Benjamin called out, and he and Calvin let go.

Daniel tucked himself and hit the water—with enough force to get the men above him good and wet, he hoped. By the time he surfaced and got some air into his lungs a rope had already been lowered. "You two just wait 'til I get my hands on ya!" he sputtered.

He heard a shuffle of feet—Benjamin and Calvin running away as usual. But then there was an unfamiliar succession of thuds, grunts and groans. Now what was *that* about?

Daniel grabbed the rope and expertly climbed out of the well. The sight that greeted him made him fall silent for a second, then pushed him into hysterics. Spencer Riley, Nowhere's sheriff, and Harlan had a hold of Benjamin, while Clayton Riley and Tom Turner were restraining Calvin.

"What do you think, Daniel?" Harlan asked. "Do your brothers need a little dip too?"

"Well, now," Daniel said. "I think it'd do 'em a heap of good to have a li'l afternoon bath."

"This is *not* how this is supposed to go!" Calvin shouted in protest.

Clayton gave him a friendly punch in the gut. "You've been tossing your brother down that well for years. I think he deserves this moment, don't you?"

"You're triflin' with *tradition*!" Calvin rasped.

"Yeah, this is how we Weavers've always done thin's," Benjamin added. "That's why it's called a tradition."

"Well, what say we expand that tradition?" Harlan winked at Spencer as they started to drag Benjamin toward the well. Tom and Clayton did likewise with their prisoner.

Daniel cackled with glee. "Didn't I always tell ya that one day ya'd get yers?"

Benjamin started laughing despite himself. "No fair, no fair!"

"Consider this a wedding present, Daniel!" Harlan called out as they tossed Benjamin over the side.

There was a huge splash, followed by "Woo-ee! Dang, this is cold!"

Daniel leaned over the side of the well. "That ain't nothin'! Remember when ya tossed me in the day after Christmas? I broke through a skin of ice that time!"

Now it was Calvin's turn. He too fought against the men holding him, but couldn't help laughing as his brother had. "I'm gonna get ya for this, Daniel!"

Daniel grinned ear to ear and held his arms out wide. "Get me for what? I'm not the one throwin' ya in!"

"He's got a point there," Clayton said as he and Tom tossed Calvin in. Another splash, though smaller than Benjamin made. Then, silence.

All five men quickly glanced at each other, then peered over the side of the well.

"You two all right down there?" Harlan called.

"Good God A'mighty," Calvin screeched. "This'll like to freeze me solid!"

Daniel rolled his eyes. "They're fine."

No sooner had he said it than Benjamin started to climb out, a silly grin on his face. "Ma's gonna kill us if'n she finds out what we…oh. Hi, Ma."

The men slowly turned around to find Ma Weaver,

her arms folded across her chest as she tapped one foot on the ground. She glared at each of them in turn as Calvin began his ascent. "What have you got to say for yourselves, gentlemen?"

Each and every man audibly gulped.

Harlan stepped forward, took off his hat and began to nervously turn it in his hands. "Er…well, myself and the other lawmen came across your twins here giving the groom-to-be a soaking. They said it was a tradition of sorts. And being the law, we felt that the punishment should fit the crime, so…"

"So we were startin' a new tradition," Benjamin quickly added.

At this point Calvin reached the top and fell out onto the grass, his breathing heavy from the climb. "By golly if that wasn't kind of fun, though."

"Though maybe the punishment should be more severe if they're enjoying it," Spencer suggested.

Benjamin, not wanting to suffer further, kicked Calvin in the hip to silence him.

It didn't work. "Ow! What did ya do that for?"

Ma marched over to him and kicked him in the other hip. "Get up, Calvin! You want your wife to see you acting like such a fool?" She turned and glared at the rest of them. "And that goes for the lot of you! You're grown men—you all know better! I've got a mind to tan all of your hides until WHAAA!"

The men laughed as Harlan scooped her up into his arms and headed off. "What in tarnation are you doing, Harlan Hughes?!" she screeched.

"Having some fun, woman," he said as he aimed for the barn.

Her three sons began to laugh as she struggled. "That's showin' her, Harlan!" Benjamin called after him.

"Harlan, you put me down right this instant!"

"I will—just as soon as we get where we're going."

"And where is that?" she snapped.

Harlan lowered his voice to a whisper. "Someplace where I can kiss you proper!"

Ma thought she would die of embarrassment. And she would have, if she hadn't been enjoying herself so much. "You'll do no such thing!"

"Oh, won't I?" Harlan said. "Even though it's a long time coming?"

"Why you, you…" were the last words the Weaver men and the others heard her speak as Sheriff Hughes entered the barn.

"Ya don't think she'll hurt him, do ya?" Calvin asked.

"Nah, they're fine," Benjamin said.

"Ain't folks gonna think it's improper that Sheriff Hughes is sparkin' with your ma in the barn?" Deputy Turner asked.

Daniel shook his head. "They've been sweet on each other for years now. Let the man propose any way he wants."

"Propose?" Clayton and Spencer said in unison.

"Well, I'll be," Deputy Turner drawled. "How did I not know he was sweet on your ma?"

"No idea," said Calvin. "We've known for ages. Though she'd have rather died than say it."

Benjamin smiled at Daniel. "Ya know, little brother, ya might not be the only one gettin' hitched tomorrow…"

Meanwhile, in the barn…

"Ow! Tarnation, woman, what are you trying to do, skewer me? Put down that pitchfork!"

"I'll put it down when I'm good and ready! Now what do you mean, hauling me in here like a sack of grain?"

"Don't you know a romantic gesture when you see one?" he shot back.

"Sheriff Hughes, plucking a woman off the ground and running away with her is not a *romantic* notion!"

"Great Scott, woman, haven't you ever read poetry?" Harlan threw up his hands. "For crying out loud, you've got four sons! You must've had some sense of romance to bring them about!"

Mary gasped. "That is none of your business, *Sheriff*!"

Harlan stared at her a moment. Her face was red, her body trembling from her earlier struggles. She was fire on two legs, and had a way of setting his blood to boiling. Harlan never thought he'd love anyone ever again, but he was wrong. Now he had to fix this. "Mary… what happened to calling me Harlan?" he asked gently.

She lowered the pitchfork a notch. "You can't go around doing what you just did."

He smiled. "I think you liked it."

"I did not like it!"

"I think you did."

"What makes you so sure?" she asked as her eyes narrowed to slits.

He took a few steps forward, but still kept some distance between them, for safety's sake. "Because I know that when you're really mad you get quiet. You don't take to hollering like you're doing now."

She took a deep breath. He was right, of course, and they both knew it. She trembled anew, but not from her earlier exertions. Now she trembled because of the man himself. "Oh, what do you know?"

"Plenty." He closed the distance between them, pulled the pitchfork from her hands and tossed it at a pile of hay. "Mary…"

She backed up a few steps. "Harlan… I…that is, we…"

"Don't fight me, woman," he said quietly. "We're both old enough to know better. Now I'm just gonna say it right out. I love you, Mary Weaver, I've loved you for a long time and I'll be powerful upset if you say no."

She swallowed hard. "No to what?"

Harlan got down on one knee.

"Oh, sweet Lord above!" Mary gasped.

Harlan cleared his throat. "Mary Weaver, you'd make me the happiest old coot alive if you'd be my wife." He stared at her and waited.

Mary stared right back. It took her a moment to find her voice and when she did, all she could say was, "You're not an old coot." Then she fled from the barn.

Chapter Twelve

"Ma?" Charity said with a raised eyebrow as Ma burst through the kitchen's back door, crossed the room to the hallway and disappeared. She exchanged a quick look with Ebba.

"Is something wrong?" Ebba asked.

"I'm not sure." Charity stepped away from the stove to peek down the hallway. "But she didn't seem right."

"Maybe one of us should check on her," Ebba suggested.

"You go," Charity said. "I've got to take these pies out of the oven."

Ebba wiped her hands on her apron and left the kitchen. She had a feeling she'd find Ma in the sewing room. Sure enough, there she was at her worktable, stabbing at a hat with a long needle. "Ma? Is everything all right?"

"Everything's fine, child," she replied in a voice indicating it clearly wasn't. "How are the pies coming along?"

"The pies are fine. But if you don't mind me saying so, you're not."

Ma fiddled with the half-made hat on the worktable. She closed her eyes and shook her head. "Men! Pigheaded fools."

"What are you talking about?"

Ma gasped as she turned to look at her. "Oh, Ebba, I'm sorry. I didn't mean for it to come out sounding like that."

"Are you…mad at someone?"

Ma sighed. "If I'm upset with anyone, it's myself. In fact, I just did something that might not have been the brightest, considering the circumstances."

"What circumstances?" Ebba asked. "What happened?"

Ma sat back in her chair and seemed to crumple. "Did you ever want something, then when it came along you discovered you were too scared to take it?"

Ebba thought a moment. "Yes, I think so."

"What was it?"

Ebba gave her a tentative smile. "Your son."

"Daniel?" Ma said, sitting bolt upright. "Land sakes, child, why would you be afraid of Daniel?"

"Well…he's a stranger, yes, but I'll get to know him over time…and I've always wanted to be married and have a family. But there are no guarantees anything will work out, is there?"

"What are you talking about, child?"

"I'm talking about, what if we never fall in love? You know, what you were telling me the other day?

Those three things I have to have in my pocket? What if I only ever get two and never find the third?"

Ma sighed again. "Child, you're young, and with two in your pocket the third is bound to come along. But at my age…it's more difficult."

Ebba suddenly knew what was going on. "Sheriff Hughes."

Ma's mouth dropped open. "How do you know about…"

"Daniel told me. In fact, all of your sons know that the sheriff and you—as they put it—'have eyes for each other.'"

Ma rested her elbows on the worktable and put her face in her hands. "I never thought this would happen to me," she muttered into her fingers. "I never thought I'd find it again." She looked up. "And now here it is and I don't know what to do with it."

Ebba came around the worktable and sat in a nearby chair. "If it were me, what advice would you give?"

"Oh, now that's not fair," Ma objected, then chuckled. "You'll make a Weaver yet, Ebba."

Ebba smiled at her. "What would you tell me? What should I do?"

"I'd ask you if you liked him, loved him and were in love with him."

Ebba leaned forward. "Are you?"

Ma's lower lip trembled. "For a while now, yes."

Ebba was surprised at the tears streaming down Ma's cheeks. She scooted her chair closer and took the woman's hands in hers. "What's wrong, Ma? He seems like a very good man. And if he loves you too, then…"

"He does!" Ma blurted. "He just told me so!"

"Then I don't understand. Why are you in here crying while he's out there somewhere?"

Ma gave her a helpless look. "Because I'm afraid, child. I'm afraid I'll...oh, never mind." She quickly wiped the tears from her eyes and stood. "You'd best go back and help Charity with those pies."

"I will not," Ebba stated.

Ma gaped at her. "Go back to the kitchen, Ebba. Please."

Ebba got up and took Ma in her arms. "No. You need me here."

Ma choked back a sob. "Dagnabit, girl, why can't you listen?"

"Because I'm trying to be like you," Ebba whispered and hugged her tighter. "You're a strong woman, Ma, one I can aspire to. It's not like you to run from anything. If *you* run from it, then that means it'll be too scary for *me* to face."

Ma gently pushed them apart and stared at her in wonderment. "Lord, child, you're wiser than I thought." She swallowed hard and sat. "You're right, I have to face this whether I want to or not. I just wish I knew why I'm so afraid of it."

Ebba retook her seat as well. "Maybe because you never thought it would happen."

"No, I don't think that's it."

Ebba stared at the hats on the worktable then glanced around the room. "Maybe because you don't want to replace your sons' father with a new one?"

Ma closed her eyes against more tears and nodded.

"Ebba, you truly are wise beyond your years. Now let's not talk about it anymore. You go help Charity with those pies—I'll join you in a minute."

Ebba watched Ma out of the corner of her eye for the next hour as they, Charity, and Summer and Elle Riley (Clayton's and Spencer's wives) worked in the kitchen. Rufi managed the Riley children while the women baked.

"How old is little Charlie now, Summer?" Ma asked.

Summer stopped kneading dough to think. She and Elle were both pretty blondes with bright blue eyes and soft Louisiana accents—they'd grown up as best friends in New Orleans. "Four and a half now," she finally said.

"And his sister?" Ma inquired.

"Kate just turned two."

"They're both dears," Ma said with a smile. "I'm sure they give Leona hours of pleasure. As you can see, there's no shortage of it around here with the amount of children we've got."

Elle laughed. "Honestly, Mrs. Weaver, I don't know how you do it. You have children coming out of every nook and cranny."

"Just how I like it," Ma said. "Summer, how's that pie dough coming?"

"It's ready to be rolled out," she said, reaching for a rolling pin.

"And what about you, Elle?" Ma turned to her. "How old are Fletcher and Clementine?"

"Fletcher is three; Clementine just turned one."

"My, I didn't realize Kate and Clementine's birthdays were so close together," Ma said.

"Only two weeks apart," Summer said as she began to roll out her dough.

"Are you looking forward to having children, Ebba?" Elle asked.

The room went silent for a moment. "Ebba?" Charity said. "Did you hear Elle?"

Ebba jumped. She'd been so busy watching Ma, she hadn't realized someone was addressing her. "Oh… sorry, what was the question?"

Elle smiled as if she understood her distraction. "I asked if you're looking forward to having children."

Ebba blushed. "To tell you the truth, right now the only thing I'm looking forward to is getting through tonight and tomorrow."

A series of giggles made its way around the kitchen. "One thing at a time, then," Summer said. "I must say though, I am jealous."

"Jealous? Of what?" Ebba asked.

"That you get to have wedding guests."

"You didn't have any at your wedding?" Ebba asked.

"Nothing like what you'll have."

"Summer got married the night of Christmas Eve," Elle explained. "She only had six or eight people present. When I married Spencer, it was a full church wedding plus an extra bride and groom—Billy Blake married Abbey Davis at the same time!"

Summer shook her head as she started to roll out the dough. "That was an event, to say the least."

"How many people were at your wedding, Charity?" Ebba asked.

"Let me see…the Weavers, the preacher and Aunt Betsy. That was all."

"Isn't it amazing that you remember all these details?" Ma asked. "They fade, but then one day everything is as clear as a painting on the wall again. You'll do the same with your children. It's like finding a present when you didn't expect one."

The other women smiled at her. "Have you found a present lately, Ma?" Ebba asked. She figured she'd sneak that in. Ma couldn't put up too much of a fuss in front of the others, could she?

Ma gave her something between a dirty look and a smile. She knew exactly what Ebba meant. "I suppose I have."

That got everyone else's attention. Charity arched an eyebrow. "Really? Is there something I should know about?"

"Oh, it's nothing, really." Ma wiped her hands on her apron.

Ebba wanted to yank the woman's apron off and make her go talk to Sheriff Hughes, but didn't think she could pull it off.

As it turned out, she didn't need to. "Afternoon, ladies," Sheriff Hughes said as he came through the back door. "I heard something about cookies?"

"I'm sorry," Ma said, "we're busy with baking more pies for tomorrow. But there are some from yesterday." She went to the hutch where the cookie jar was and brought it to the table. "Help yourself."

"Don't mind if I do," he said as he took off the lid and pulled out a few. "Mmm, sugar cookies are one of my favorites."

"I'm afraid they won't be as good as Mrs. Upton's back in Clear Creek." Ma turned her back on him. Ebba watched her stand and fold her arms across her chest. Heavens, the woman was stubborn!

"Now, I wouldn't say that, Mary," the sheriff argued. "Your sugar cookies are as good as Sally Upton's any day."

"Are they?" she asked as she glanced over her shoulder at him.

"Of course they are. Sally might be the hotel's cook and make some fabulous meals, but it's her molasses cookies that are tough to beat."

Ebba wanted to bury her face in her hands. Did he have to say that?

Ma spun to face him. "Oh they are, are they?"

The sheriff backed up a step. "What'd I say?"

"Take your cookies and scoot!" Ma ordered as she grabbed the cookie jar and shoved it back in the hutch.

"Ma, you forgot the lid," Charity said, pointing at it.

Ma grunted, snatched up the lid, took it to the hutch and put it back on the cookie jar. Then she spun on her heel to face Harlan. "Don't be taking up space in the kitchen, Sheriff—we've got a lot of work to do."

"As do we menfolk. What did you want us to do with those crates in the barn?"

"Why don't you ask one of my boys?" she asked tersely.

He arched an eyebrow at her. "No need to get upset, Mary. None of the boys are around."

"What? Well, where in tarnation are they?"

"How should I know?" he said with a helpless shrug. "If I did, you think I'd be in here asking you?"

She didn't budge an inch. "Well, Sheriff, I'm rather busy right now and I don't need distractions." The look on her face said exactly what kind of distraction she meant.

The other women cast nervous glances between the two. "Do you want one of us to go find them?" Charity asked.

"No," Ma snapped. "They're probably trying to finish up the plowing so they don't have to worry about getting behind."

The sheriff looked at the cookies in his hand. "Where did you want me to put the crates, Mary?"

Ebba decided to take charge. "Maybe you'd better go show him, Ma." She gave her a nudge toward the door.

Ma gave her a *what do you think you're doing?* look before turning back to the sheriff. "I…well…"

"That's a good idea," Charity added. "How is the sheriff supposed to know where to put them unless you tell him?"

"Go ahead, take care of it while we get finished up in here," a grinning Summer suggested.

Ebba fought against a smile. *Thank you, ladies!*

Ma pressed her lips together before she conceded. "All right, Harlan, follow me."

"So that's what's wrong," Charity said.

Ebba smiled and nodded.

"Sheriff Hughes and Mrs. Weaver," Elle said in wonder. "Who'd have thought?"

"Her entire family, apparently," Summer replied.

"Well, enough thinking for now," Charity declared. "Let's get this last batch of pies in the oven, then we can start on the cookies."

Summer and Elle nodded in agreement and continued with their tasks as Ebba wondered what to do next. Maybe she should ready herself for when Ma came back in the house. Judging from what she knew of the woman so far, she'd either be upset again or smiling.

But there was no time to ponder it further, as several children came racing through the kitchen and out the back door. "Heavens, what's the hurry?"

"Rufi?" Charity called into the next room.

Rufi dashed into the kitchen, her eyes darting everywhere. "Where did they go, the little *ladri*?!"

"That way," Ebba said and pointed at the door.

"Who were they?" Summer asked.

"Gabby, Leo and Mel," Rufi spat. "My younger brother and sisters."

"Why were they in such a rush?" Ebba asked.

"Because the devils just took my necklace and they know I can't catch them to get it back," Rufi said with a roll of her eyes. She sat down heavily at the kitchen table to catch her breath. "But I'll get it back later. They just want me to chase them, the *fuorileggi*."

Summer's son Charlie came running into the room. "Chase me, chase me!" he cried as he ran around the kitchen table and back into the hall.

Rufi took a deep breath as if to brace herself, stood

up and ran back into the parlor. Her arrival was greeted with a cacophony of giggles and squeals of delight.

Ebba couldn't help but laugh. She took a deep breath herself and realized how tired she felt. She wasn't used to being around so many people, at least not in the same house. Once again she found herself thinking about the peace and quiet to come after the wedding was over and the guests were gone. Unfortunately, she still wouldn't be alone. By her estimation there were twenty-four other people living on the farm. If Sheriff Hughes had his way, it would be twenty-five. Egads, twenty-six if she included herself!

The thought made her head swim. After the wedding, she'd have to talk to Daniel about them building a house of their own, before she went mad from the crowds.

"Ebba, are you all right?" Charity asked.

"I'm fine. Just a little tired from all the excitement, I guess."

"And no wonder," Summer added. "I remember when a few folks stayed the night at the farm because of the snow when Clayton and I got married. But there weren't nearly as many people at my wedding as yours."

"And she doesn't have the luxury of walking out of the church and going home," Elle added. "She is home."

"Maybe you should go upstairs and lie down," Charity offered.

Ebba glanced at each of them. Would they think less of her if she took Charity up on her offer? She should stay and help...yet on the other hand, a few moments to herself would be heavenly. "Are you sure?"

All three women nodded. "Enjoy it while you can," Elle said. "From the looks of things, a moment to yourself is going to be a rare thing around here."

Ebba's heart sank at the statement. Just as she'd been thinking… "Thank you," she told them, then headed upstairs.

Once in her room, she sighed in relief and went to the window. She pushed back the lace curtain and gazed out upon the orchards below. Daniel's room was at the front of the house and had a wonderful view of the apple trees and the little valley beyond. She noticed a wagon coming over the top of the rise and watched as it began its descent down to the farmhouse.

"More people," she said to herself. "I wonder who." She didn't have to wait long to find out—as soon as the wagon got close enough, she was able to spot the pig. The Davises had arrived.

Chapter Thirteen

Ebba knew she should go downstairs but couldn't muster the energy. Now that she was alone, everything she'd been through since arriving in Denver was catching up to her: her parents' death, working for horrible Mrs. Feldnick, meeting with Mrs. Pettigrew, the long trip, the ideas she'd had in her head about Daniel and his family, not to mention the expectations she'd set up...

None of those expectations remotely resembled the situation she found herself in—except for her allergies flaring up in the countryside, of course. That one, she'd hit the bull's-eye.

She was surrounded by people here, almost two-dozen future relatives, and would continue to be for as long as she was married to this man. She was expected to work as hard as they did, from before sunup to after sundown, even in the fields. But that wasn't what bothered her most. What did was that Daniel had accepted her ailment like it was nothing. He was willing to look past it and take her "as is."

Ebba swallowed hard. The question was, was she willing to do the same for him and his family? Did she have the same fortitude to jump into this marriage with both feet as Daniel? Sure, mail-order brides and their grooms were strangers at the onset. But Daniel's willingness to accept her while knowing she wasn't the best candidate for farm life made it all seem—how should she put it—too good to be true? Yes, that was it.

But would he still accept her later, when she was unable to do the work required of her because of her constant sneezing?

She shook her head as she watched a portly, middle-aged man bring the wagon to a stop in front of the house, set the brake and climb down. He walked around the horses to get to the other side of the wagon and help his wife do the same while Matthew and his wife Charlotte maneuvered around the pig to disembark. She saw Mrs. Davis look at everything with either indifference or disapproval.

Ebba glanced at the orchards and wondered why the woman couldn't or wouldn't appreciate the simple beauty of the little valley. Then again, maybe Mrs. Davis felt that when you'd seen one farm, you'd seen them all. Or maybe she just liked looking down on things. Based on meeting her back in Nowhere, that was a possibility.

Ebba went back to the bed, falling backwards onto the mattress and staring at the ceiling. The men would be coming into the house soon. What would they do for supper with all these extra people here? More would arrive tomorrow before the wedding. Then the Weavers would really have a houseful!

Ebba threw an arm over her eyes and tried not to think about it. No wonder Ma was on edge. Sheriff Hughes hadn't chosen the best time to profess his love for the woman, even if the farm was taking on the atmosphere of a wedding celebration. Maybe that's what prompted him to choose to do so, but her reaction couldn't have been what he hoped for.

But then, what would she do or say on the day Daniel did the same? She let her arm slide onto the mattress. "Daniel…" she whispered. "Daniel." She liked the sound of his name. "I love you." But there was no heart behind her words, because they weren't true. She didn't love him, and wasn't sure she could.

"Ohhhh, why do I always have to think like this?" She sat up and folded her hands in her lap. Was she getting cold feet? "If I am, that's not going to do me much good." No, indeed. Where would she go? What would she do? If the man she would marry tomorrow was confident they were going to be good together, then why couldn't she be?

Because there are no guarantees, that's why, she thought to herself. *And once you're married to this man, there's no turning back…*

Ebba took a deep breath and blew it out. "Why did I ever think I could become a mail-order bride?" she asked aloud. But then, what options did she have? It had been that or a lifetime of drudgery under the hectoring voice of Mrs. Feldnick. Better to marry a stranger—

heck, better to die alone in the wilderness—than live under the thumb of that old biddy.

She sighed again and felt pathetic for doing so. What was wrong with her? What was she so afraid of? At least one of them was sure they'd be happy.

She smiled as she remembered the look on Daniel's face as he held her in his arms on the porch swing. *"You and I are gonna be okay,"* he'd said. She could hear the smile in his voice and feel the surety of his words while in his arms. It was in that moment, miserable with her stuffy nose and watery eyes, that she believed him, if only briefly. How was she able to do it? She didn't know.

Ebba only knew that she wanted to believe him again and hang on to that belief. The last thing she wanted to start her marriage out with was a bucketful of doubt. Right now, however, she felt like she had one of those buckets in each hand to carry down the aisle. Worse, she didn't know how to let go.

By the time supper rolled around the Weaver house was filled to the brim with people. Calvin, Bella and their—for lack of a better term—tribe were everywhere. Arlan, Samijo and their children, along with Ma, the Quinns and the Davises, took up the dining parlor, while the Rileys, Benjamin and Charity and their son were in the kitchen. Sheriff Hughes, Daniel, Ebba and Truly (for the life of her, Ebba didn't know how she wound up with the baby in her lap) were on the front porch.

The sheriff had taken the crates and placed them

around the house and porch so people could use them as chairs. Daniel had also brought chairs down from some of the bedrooms. Everyone sat and visited, and when the notion took them, got up and went into the kitchen for chicken and biscuits.

It was noisy, it was loud and Nellie Davis's occasional gasp of shock was the only interruption to the cacophony of laughter, shouting, backslapping, children crying and the clinking of dishes. *Good heavens,* Ebba thought at one point. *What was the actual wedding supper going to be like?* She certainly hoped it didn't rain! She couldn't imagine trying to stuff any more people into the house.

"We're going to have to get up mighty early to get that cake done, girls," Leona declared as she stepped onto the front porch with Ma and Betsy.

"So long as we all pitch in, we'll have it baked up right quick, Leona," Betsy said. "You don't have to worry. I'd be more concerned about that pig getting done in time."

Nellie Davis must have the hearing of an elephant, Ebba thought. In a flash she appeared in the doorway. "Don't you worry none about that pig. My husband will have it roasted to perfection by the time we're ready to eat."

"As long as it's done, that's all that matters," Ma said, then turned to Ebba. "And by the way, I moved the dress from the sewing room to your room, child."

"Thank you, Ma," Ebba said with a smile.

Nellie eyed her fellow matrons and raised an eyebrow. "Well?"

"Deep subject," Harlan muttered. Daniel suppressed a snort.

"Well what?" Betsy asked, ignoring the men.

"Aren't you going to show it to us?" Nellie asked, as if accusing someone of hiding something.

"The dress?" Ma said. "Ebba, do you mind?"

"No, I don't mind."

"Then why don't you take her upstairs and show it to her? In fact, I'm sure Charlotte would love to see it as well."

"If'n you can find Charlotte," Daniel said with a smile. "I ain't seen her for a while. Matthew wandered out here a few minutes ago, though."

"Never mind about Matthew," Nellie said with a roll of her eyes. "Why would he be interested in seeing a wedding dress?"

"Dunno," Daniel said with a laugh. "But seein' as how it's *my* bride, I cain't wait!"

Ebba blushed as she got up from her chair, passed the baby to Daniel and headed into the house. Nellie followed her up the stairs without a word. It made Ebba nervous and she quickened her step. "It's in here," she said as she opened the door. Ma had hung it on the armoire, freshly ironed and looking beautiful. In fact, every time Ebba saw it, a thrill of excitement went up her spine. It was too bad she'd only get to wear it once.

"Well, will you look at that," Nellie said. "I must say, Miss Knudsen, I didn't expect someone like you to have a dress like this. Did you make it yourself?"

Ebba's eyebrows rose in curiosity. What did she

mean, *someone like you*? "No, I didn't. It was given to me."

"A hand-me-down, I take it?"

Ebba briefly pressed her lips together before she spoke. "A gift."

"How nice. From your...employer, perhaps?"

"Employer? No, from Mrs. Pettigrew at the bridal agency."

"Well, your Mrs. Pettigrew is quite generous. I can't imagine giving such a frock away, even if it is...used." She fingered the fabric, then looked at Ebba. "And you didn't have to give Mrs. Pettigrew anything in return?"

"One usually doesn't when it's a gift."

Nellie looked her up and down. "That wasn't what I meant, but that's none of your concern."

Why was this woman acting so strangely? "Is there something wrong, Mrs. Davis?"

She turned away from the dress and crossed the room to the window. "You know I must commend you, Miss Knudsen. Never in my life have I known a girl to be so...shall we say, *bold* in your intentions toward your husband?"

"Bold?" Ebba echoed. "And he won't become my husband until tomorrow afternoon."

"Of course," Nellie agreed. "All the same, you're not one to mince words."

Ebba blinked at her in confusion. "I'm sorry, but I don't know what you mean."

Nellie smirked. "Of course not. Well, it's a lovely dress, Miss Knudsen, and I'm sure you'll be very lovely in it."

The woman wasn't being forthright with her and Ebba knew it. "Is there something else you want to say to me?"

"Well," Nellie said as she went to the door. "Even though the family you're marrying into isn't the most refined and certainly not the brightest, they're still a part of Nowhere. And I must inform you that the people of Nowhere do not tolerate brazen women."

Ebba's eyes popped. "Brazen?!"

Nellie looked her up and down again. "Daniel Weaver is going to make an honest woman of you tomorrow—at least I hope he is. Try to be the wife he deserves." She marched out of the room.

Ebba stood in shock. Where had that come from? What did she mean, *brazen woman?* And what was that about Daniel making an honest woman out of her? Good heavens, it was as if she thought Ebba was some sort of a…well, she wasn't sure what exactly. She couldn't possibly be comparing her to a woman of ill repute, could she? And if so, why would she?

Ebba wrung her hands as she went to the door and puzzled over Nellie's words. "Who does that woman think she is?"

Then a thought struck. The odd looks she got in town before coming to the farm…not just the women gave her those looks, but the men too. Only the men looked at her differently: up and down, with more than a friendly gleam in their eyes…

"Brazen…" she mouthed to herself.

But why? Why would the townspeople of Nowhere assume she was a lady of the night? Had Daniel said something that led them to believe that? Perhaps she should ask him.

Then again, maybe it was just Nellie Davis. She'd heard stories from Summer and Elle earlier that day about Charlotte before she married Matthew Quinn, about the trouble she and her mother Nellie had caused them, not to mention Clayton and Spencer. But Charlotte had more than redeemed herself according to the Rileys. Perhaps her mother hadn't, though. And Sheriff Hughes had said she always had "something in her craw"…

Well, whatever was going on, she needed to find out before it went any farther. Ebba blew out a breath, squared her shoulders and went back downstairs into the chaos.

Clayton Riley hadn't been to the Weaver farm in years. He was amazed at the size of the orchards the family had grown and cultivated in their little valley. "I've got to hand it to you, Arlan," he said as they strolled into the nearest one. "You and your family have done right fine for yourselves since your pa died."

"It wasn't easy at times," Arlan said, "but we've managed."

"I can see that." Clayton's eyes slowly drifted to the setting sun. "May I ask you something?"

"Of course." Arlan turned to watch the sunset. "What's on yer mind?"

"I don't want this to sound wrong, or offend you, but…some of the folks in town have been talking about Daniel's bride."

Arlan's head slowly rotated toward him. "Have they now? And just what are they sayin'?"

"Well, I myself overheard several women in the mercantile wonder about her past, that it might not be something one would expect in a bride."

Arlan's brow furrowed. "Expect? Or want?"

"The latter, actually. I'm not saying this to upset you or your family. I'm saying it so Daniel can have a chance to speak with her before they get hitched tomorrow. That way when they venture into town, folks giving them funny looks won't come as no surprise."

"What do ya mean? Just what are folks sayin' about her? Be specific, Clayton. We've known each other for too long for ya to go around in circles."

"I'm not going in circles, I'm just giving you what little I know. But it's enough to make me think your brother should know too."

"Then what're ya doin' standin' here talkin' to me when ya should be talkin' to Daniel?"

"Because I think he'd take it better if it came from you."

Arlan put his hands on his hips. "So what yer tellin' me is folks in town are sayin' my brother's future bride is damaged goods?"

"That's what's being said, or something along those lines." Clayton took off his hat and slapped it against his leg. "Maybe I shouldn't have said anything. I'm sorry, Arlan."

"Nah, if folks are talkin', then they had to've heard somethin'. That means someone started flappin' their gums about her. How else could they hear anythin'?"

Clayton nodded. "I'll give you two guesses. First one don't count."

"Nellie Davis," Arlan groaned.

"But without any proof, who's to say? I did ask a few folks, but they didn't seem too eager to tell me."

"Of course not, Clayton. Yer not a woman." Arlan turned back to the sunset. "What are the men saying?"

"Not what the women are. But they're not telling me much either. A couple of them were sitting at a corner table in Hank's the other day, saying how lucky they thought Daniel was."

"Lucky? How's marrying a woman with loose morals, if that's what they're insinuatin', lucky?"

"I'd like to know why Nellie started such a rumor in the first place," Clayton mused. "I thought she'd gotten past that sort of thing. The only thing I can think of is because Ebba's new in town. But that's no reason. Nellie wouldn't do something like that just because she was bored."

"Ya sure of that?"

Clayton looked at Arlan for a moment before reluctantly replying, "Not entirely."

Arlan offered Clayton his hand. "Regardless, I'm much obliged ya told me."

Clayton gave it a shake. "It's been on my mind, Arlan. I just figured you ought to know so you can tell your brother before he makes any trips to town with her."

Arlan nodded. "Don't worry, I'll tell him. The rest will be up to him."

"And if Benjamin and Charity don't want to build their own house," Daniel said, "Ebba and I can build one on the back acres near the creek."

Harlan and Mr. Davis listened intently to Daniel's plans. "I would think that your brother Benjamin would want to build a house," said Mr. Davis. "After all, he and his wife already have children. They obviously need the room more than you do."

"True enough, Mr. Davis, and they might just do that." Daniel glanced at the sheriff. "'Course, a lot depends on how many folks'll be livin' in the main house."

Harlan cleared his throat and shifted his weight. "That old house has had a lot of people come through it lately."

Daniel grinned. "Sure enough has, Sheriff. This here's a mighty fine place to work and live. And, for folks like my brothers and me, a great place to raise younguns. 'Course, it's also a nice place for a gentleman of yer…maturity to settle."

"Are you referring to our age, Danny boy?" Mr. Davis said with a laugh. "A fine thing when all you young men are doing the work."

"Yeah, we're doin' the work, but there's other work to be done too. Take Ma, for example…"

The sheriff cleared his throat again and stuck his hands in his pockets. "Your mama is one of the hardest-working women I've ever met."

"That's just it," Daniel said. "It'd be great if she had someone around to help her out."

"She has all of you boys," Mr. Davis pointed out. "And your wives."

"I mean someone to keep her company. Make sure no lowdown snake comes sneakin' into the house to do her harm. Someone she can go to town with and who'll look after her." Both he and Mr. Davis looked at the sheriff.

Harlan glanced between the two. "All right! If you must know, yes, I asked your ma to marry me!"

"Ya don't hafta tell me, Sheriff," Daniel said. "Anyone with half the brain of a squirrel coulda figgered that out."

The sheriff blanched. "How did you know…?"

"'Cause Ma was actin' funny around ya come supper time. Me and my brothers figgered if'n she was tryin' To avoid ya, she must really like ya!"

Mr. Davis slapped the sheriff on the back. "Congratulations, Harlan!"

"Don't congratulate me yet," he said.

"Why not?" Daniel and Mr. Davis asked at once.

"Because she hasn't said yes. And for all I know, she never will."

Chapter Fourteen

Ebba tossed and turned all night. She'd barely drifted off when Charity knocked on her door, opened it and poked her head inside. "Best get up. We have a lot to do before we get you into that dress."

Ebba sat up and stretched. This would be a long day. She knew more people were arriving, but couldn't remember who. Was it more relatives? Probably, but whom did they belong to—the Quinns, the Weavers or the Rileys? And she still didn't know what Nellie Davis had been nattering on about. Brazen? She was about as brazen as a nun!

Well, no hope for it. She'd just have to get up, get ready and face the day. She'd find out when she found out.

She went to the washstand and started her morning routine. After she dressed and braided her hair, she wrapped the braids around her head and pinned them in place, then studied herself in the washstand's small mirror. "Ebba Knudsen, by tonight you'll be Ebba Weaver."

A sudden commotion downstairs caught her attention. It sounded like a herd of buffalo was coming up the stairs. Bella and Calvin must have arrived.

Ebba looked back at her reflection. "Lord have mercy on me," she said just as Bella's younger siblings ran into her room, some of them colliding into each other in the doorway and falling in instead.

Gabby climbed over Arturo and Leonardo, then ran to her. "I want to see your dress, I want to see your dress!"

Ebba pointed to where it hung from the armoire. "It's right there."

The children turned and gawked at it. "It's so pretty," Mel said in awe. She looked at Ebba. "Bella could make one just like it. She's very good at it. I hope I'm as good at sewing as my sister one day."

Rufi burst into the room, clearly out of breath. "I'm…sorry, Ebba…but they got away from me."

The boys cringed and backed up a step. Ebba caught the action and eyed them. "What did they do?"

"They tied Rufi to a tree!" Gabby squealed and laughed.

Ebba gasped. "That's terrible!" She immediately looked at Rufi to confirm the accusation.

Rufi rolled her eyes and half-heartedly threw her hands in the air. "At least they don't know how to tie good knots."

Ebba spun on the boys. "That was an awful thing to do!"

"We didn't mean to do it," Leo said in their defense.

"Oh yes, you did," Gabby countered.

Lucia, the one sibling of Bella's Ebba hadn't spoken with yet, smiled shyly before making a face at her brothers.

Ebba folded her arms in front of her. "You can't *accidentally* tie someone to a tree. So…what do you have to say for yourselves?"

"We just wanted to see how fast Rufi could get loose," Alfonso said, winking at Lucia.

"He's lying," Mel said flatly. "They thought *Nonna* made cinnamon bread this morning because it's your wedding day and wanted to get to it before it was all gone."

"Yeah," Gabby agreed. "They knew Rufi would make us wait until all the grown-ups had theirs first."

"But we weren't sure there'd be any left!" Arturo whined. "*Nonna*'s cinnamon bread is so wonderful, it practically melts in your mouth! We love it!"

"So you thought that if you tied your sister to a tree, you'd get some before anyone else?" Ebba asked, trying to keep her scowl in place.

The younger children nodded and giggled.

The older ones looked at Rufi—and realized she'd blocked their only escape route. She was standing in the doorway, feet apart and hands on her hips. "Well, what do you have to say for yourselves? You know you shouldn't be pulling these sorts of pranks on Ebba's wedding day!"

"We're sorry, Rufi," Arturo said, his head hung low. "We won't do it again."

"That's right you won't," she said. "Because I'm telling *Nonna*."

The look of terror on the boys' faces emboldened Ebba. "And so am I. I'm also telling her you ran into a woman's room without knocking."

"No! No!" Alfonso begged. "We'll be good the rest of the day! We promise!"

"You better," Rufi warned. "Today is not the day for childish pranks."

Ebba felt a sudden tugging of her skirt. She bent down and looked at Gabby. "What is it?"

"Don't worry, Ebba, we won't tie you to a tree," Gabby said innocently before kissing her on the cheek. "If we did, you couldn't marry Daniel."

Ebba laughed despite herself. "I'm relieved to know that. And don't tie Daniel to a tree either, or there still won't be a wedding."

"Does that mean you won't tell *Nonna* on us?" Leo asked hopefully.

Ebba pursed her lips as she straightened. "Maybe."

"All right, downstairs, all of you *facinorosi*!" Rufi began to wave the children toward the door. "Get some breakfast. Then I'm sure *Nonna* will have some work for you... I hope."

Ebba watched the children file out the door, but stopped Rufi before she followed. "Did they really tie you to a tree?"

"It's not the first time. And I *am* telling *Nonna*, because I'm tired of it, especially on a day like this. Besides, they're starting to get good at it."

Ebba's eyes widened. "Oh my goodness!" she said with a laugh. "Well, I'll back you up, don't worry."

Rufi shook her head. "They get more mischievous

by the day. I would hope the older ones would have grown out of it by now, but *Zii* Benjamin and Calvin teach them things."

"What kinds of things?" Ebba asked as she headed for the door. She knew they couldn't linger for much longer. It was her wedding day, after all.

"The little ones, they hide my shoes. The older boys, they put frogs in my bed and pepper in my tea. *Buon Dio omnipotente!*"

Ebba tried to imagine the patience the girl must have. "Don't Calvin and Bella discipline them?"

"Bella is busy with her children. Calvin is out working all day. That leaves me to look after them," Rufi concluded tiredly.

"What about school? Lessons? Doesn't that occupy most of the day?"

"It would, if there was someone to teach them." Rufi's eyes drifted to the floor. "I can teach a few things but… I don't read and write as well as I should."

"I'm sorry, Rufi. I didn't realize the burden you had with them. Maybe I can help."

"But of course you will. Calvin and Bella said so."

"They…did? What did they say?"

"That you're going to teach me and the others how to read, write and speak better English."

"What?" Ebba said and took a step back. "When did she tell you that?" *And why didn't they tell* me *that*, she added mentally.

"After Daniel told Bella what you put in your letter, that you could read and write well and do your numbers." Rufi's eyes went to the floor again. "I'm not very good with numbers at all. But you'll help me, won't you?"

Ebba saw the starry expression on Rufi's face. She shook herself as the girl's words sank in. "I'll have to speak with Calvin and Bella about this. No one told me I was expected to be a schoolteacher."

Rufi's face fell. "You mean, you didn't know you were going to be our new teacher?"

Ebba closed her eyes at the first sting of anger. "Let's not talk about it right now. I'll discuss it with Daniel later."

"You look upset," Rufi pointed out.

"I'm…let's just not talk about it right now." Ebba continued downstairs, fuming. First the size of the family, then Nellie Davis's insinuations, and now this. What else had Daniel not told her?

The rest of the morning was a blur. Ebba barely knew if she was coming or going. She knew she needed to talk to Daniel—about a lot of things—but wasn't sure when she'd have a chance. Everyone was busy preparing for the ceremony, including her. How was she going to get this straightened out before they said their vows?

The more she thought about what Rufi said, the more upset she became. Daniel hadn't told her about his family, about doing farm work, about having her step in as a schoolteacher, about…whatever Nellie Davis thought. She hadn't gotten the truth from him about a lot of things. Who knew what else had "slipped his mind"? Did they expect her to deliver the mail to the Gunderson stage stop too?

"That's it," she said to herself. "I should write a letter to Mrs. Pettigrew and tell her what's going on." Had she known about this? But if she did, why didn't she tell her? Ebba wiped her hands on her apron, glanced around the busy kitchen and slipped out of the room. Maybe if she penned a quick note to Mrs. Pettigrew she'd feel better, not to mention figure out what she'd say to Daniel. She loathed the thought that her future husband might be lying to her, but what was she supposed to think?

Once upstairs in her room, she found some paper, pen and ink and set to work. The letter was short and to the point, but included everything, including the hellion children. What would she do if they tied *her* to a tree? She shuddered at the thought as she signed her name at the bottom, folded it and stuck it in her apron pocket. As soon as she could find an envelope, she'd get it ready to post. She was sure Sheriff Hughes would be more than happy to mail it for her once he got back to Nowhere.

She was about to leave the room when she heard the distinct sound of a wagon approaching. Lovely—more guests. "Who could that be?" she asked aloud. She went to the window and saw a young couple arriving, but had no idea who they might be. She shook her head, guessing she'd just have to go downstairs and find out.

Taking a deep breath, she patted the letter in her pocket and headed for the door. She had to admit, writing Mrs. Pettigrew did make her feel better. Writing her thoughts always did. Besides, Mrs. Pettigrew promised to answer any letter a bride sent to her.

Who knows what might happen between now and when she heard back, though. She certainly hoped she and Daniel would have their misunderstandings cleared up. She also hoped she didn't find herself the victim of the children's antics. The thought of a frog in her bed didn't set well.

"There you are!" Leona hurried to the bottom of the stairs. "Where have you been? We've got to get you into your wedding dress right away!"

"Oh, I'm sorry," Ebba said. "I was upstairs taking care of a few things."

"Well, now it's time to take care of the most important thing. You turn around and get right back up there. Mary, Betsy and I will be up in a moment to help you."

Ebba sighed. Would she ever get the chance to speak to Daniel before the wedding? Would she have to marry him with all this unresolved? She hoped she wasn't going to regret this. She'd known of misunderstandings that turned into something more serious. The last thing she wanted was a wedge in their relationship. He was willing to overlook her ailments for the sake of their marriage. Surely she could overlook this. Why did it gall her so?

Because he should've told you, she thought. He should've told her before they ever came out to the farm. Before she ever got on the train in Denver.

"Don't just stand there!" Leona said. "Get up those stairs and get that dress on!"

Ebba jumped. "I'm… I'm sorry. I'm going now!"

This so-called misunderstanding was bothering her more than she thought.

She hurried back to her room, closed the door and placed the dress on the bed. She glanced in the mirror and realized she looked a complete mess. Thank Heaven help was on the way. She would need it.

Just then, Leona came in with Aunt Betsy trailing behind her, a comb and brush in her hand. "Let's get to it," Betsy said with a smile. She stopped short and looked Ebba over. "Oh my, this might take a while. Maybe we should've started earlier, Leona."

"We were so busy downstairs, we lost track of the time," Leona replied. "No help for it now. Where's Mary? She has the veil."

"She'll be along in a minute," Betsy told her. "Now you sit down, Ebba, and let us take care of everything!"

Ebba was about to reply when two sets of hands grabbed her and hauled her towards the nearest chair. Before she knew it, she was sitting, a comb stuck in her hair while Leona and Aunt Betsy started to pull and tug at her clothes. "I can undress myself!" she cried. "For Heaven's sake, we'll never get anything done this way."

"She's right, Betsy," Leona said. "Let the poor child get out of her work dress—then we'll help get her into the wedding dress."

"Don't you think she ought to wash her face first?"

Leona took a closer look at Ebba. "Heavens, yes! Whatever is that goo on your cheek?"

Ebba looked in the mirror. Gabby had given her a kiss there, so it could be anything. "Let me do that first," she groaned. "Then I'll get into my dress and you can fix my hair. Would that be all right?" It came out testier than she intended.

"Yes, yes," Aunt Betsy waved her towards the screen. "Just hurry up. I knew we should've started an hour ago."

"Stop fussing, Betsy, and go fetch Mary," Leona ordered.

Betsy grumbled something unintelligible, left the room and headed downstairs.

Ebba sighed, went to the washstand and washed her face. She dried it with a towel, then turned to Leona. "I saw a young couple drive up. Who are they?"

"Warren and Bernice Johnson. Nice folks—you'll like them. Bernice comes all the way from Independence, Oregon. She was a mail-order bride too."

Ebba's brow furrowed. "Oregon? That doesn't seem very far."

"Oh, it really doesn't matter where the bride comes from, dear, so long as she gets here. Now hurry up and get out of that dress."

Ebba didn't argue, just went behind the screen to change her clothes. Leona handed her the wedding dress and helped her put it on. By the time she stepped out again, Aunt Betsy had returned with Ma. "Just look at you!" she said with a tiny clap of her hands. "Why, you're prettier now than you were the first time I saw you wearing this."

"That's because it's her wedding day," Aunt Betsy remarked. "Brides always look prettier on their wedding day."

"She'll look a lot prettier if you get her hair ready," Leona quipped as she handed her a comb.

"Don't rush me, I'll see it done." Aunt Betsy shoved Ebba back into the chair. "Oh dear, where should I begin?"

"Anywhere," Leona said. "Everyone's gathering in the orchard."

Ebba froze. "The ceremony is in the orchard?"

"Of course, dear," Leona said. "You knew that."

"Yes, but how did I forget it?" One more thing she'd have to deal with. "What if I start sneezing?!"

"The kettle's on the stove," Ma assured her. "A spot of chamomile will help you before you go out there."

"Sneezing?" Leona said.

"Didn't Mary tell you?" Betsy asked. "This poor thing suffers something awful when she goes outside."

"Oh yes, that." Leona waved a hand at her own head. "How could I forget?" She looked at Ebba and smiled. "And you thought your memory was bad?"

"Easy enough on a day like this." Betsy started to comb out Ebba's hair. "Somebody find me some pins."

"There's some on the dresser," Ebba informed them.

After a good amount of tugging and pulling, Aunt Betsy had Ebba's hair swept up into a lovely style. She stood and went to study the woman's handiwork in the mirror.

"Oh, isn't it wonderful!" Leona said with a happy smile.

"Let's put the veil on," Ma suggested.

They did, and Ebba checked her reflection again. "I… I look beautiful."

"Don't sound so surprised, dear," Leona said. "You *are* beautiful."

Ebba turned to the three matrons. "Thank you ever so much for helping me get ready." She ran a hand over the skirt of her dress, admiring it. "I had no idea I could look so nice."

"And I bet Daniel doesn't either," Ma said with a conspiratorial wink. "Now what say we have ourselves a wedding?"

Chapter Fifteen

Ebba couldn't recall how she got from her room, surrounded by three matrons helping her to prepare for her wedding, to where she was now. She stood next to Daniel's brother Arlan, one arm wrapped through his, in the middle of an orchard. The preacher from Nowhere stood at the other end, along with Daniel and his twin brothers. The people in attendance had parted to make an aisle as soon as she took Arlan's arm.

She gulped and tried not to tremble. Or breathe too much.

"All brides are nervous on their weddin' day," Arlan said in a low voice. "It shouldn't bother ya if you are too."

"It doesn't…bother me," she mumbled.

"I wouldn't hold yer breath too long if I were you. Yer face'll turn blue."

She sighed. "I can't do this."

"What do ya mean ya can't?" he said out the corner of his mouth. "Don't tell me ya changed yer mind?"

Ebba felt his arm tighten around hers, as if he was

afraid she might bolt. "No, it's not that. I want to marry your brother." *Provided he doesn't have any more secrets he's hiding from me.* "I'm just afraid I'm going to start sneezing."

"Didn't Ma fix ya some tea?"

"Yes," she said, took another short breath and held it. "But I'm worried it's not going to work."

He leaned toward her. "If ya don't start breathin' proper, yer gonna pass out."

He had a point. She let her breath out, tried to relax… and an all-too-familiar tickle teased her nose. *No…*

Suddenly, someone started playing the Wedding March on a fiddle. She glanced around to see who it was. "I didn't know Mr. Quinn played an instrument."

"Yer 'bout to be married and yer wonderin' who's playin'?" Arlan said with a smile. "Ya really are nervous. Now hush and let me walk ya down the aisle. I fancy myself a new sister-in-law."

Ebba took another breath and let him lead her toward her future husband. She looked at Daniel and saw his expression of awe. Ma was right—she *was* beautiful in Daniel's eyes.

Beautiful enough to tell the truth to? her mind asked. *Shut up*, she told it. She smiled at him, and he returned it.

Soon she and Arlan reached the end of the aisle. She stood and faced her future husband. This was it!

Arlan released her and gave her hand to Daniel. The next thing she knew, he had the other one as well, and squeezed them as they gazed at each other. "Well," he whispered, "ya ready for this?"

Ebba smiled as her misgivings slipped away. He was handsome in his Sunday best, his hair combed, his jaw clean-shaven. He even smelled heavenly—soap and pomade. He must've just bathed. He could tell her almost anything now, and she'd accept it.

She smiled and continued to stare at him as the preacher began to speak. For the first time she became utterly lost in Daniel's gaze. His eyes were locked on hers—steady, determined and seeming to reach into her very soul. She hoped he wasn't disappointed with what he saw. Heavens, she wasn't even sure what he'd see if he looked hard enough. She'd been so busy caring for her parents the last few years that maybe she'd lost sight of herself. Would Daniel see that if he kept looking into her eyes?

She tried to see into him, but faltered. What if she saw something she couldn't live with before she had to recite her vows? The worries came back in force. Would it be better to live in ignorance, or know the horrible truth only when it was too late to turn back? She longed for reassurance that she was doing the right thing, that she could give this man what he needed, that he would not betray her...

"And do you, Daniel Weaver, take this woman to be your lawfully wedded wife, to have and to hold..."

Ebba's eyes widened as the preacher continued. Good heavens, were they to that part already?

The preacher stopped, and Daniel, his eyes never wavering, smiled at her. "I do."

Good grief! she thought. *He said it! I do!*

The preacher turned to look at her, smiled and began

to recite the same thing he'd said to Daniel. He'd barely finished when "Oh no!" popped out of her mouth, right before she sneezed. And not just any sneeze…

Daniel flinched and wiped at one eye. "Woo-ee, sweetie! That was a whooper!"

Ebba thought she might die. If only the veil she wore covered her face and not just the back of her head! She sneezed again. "Don't…*achoo!*…say things like that!"

"Quick," Ma cried. "Somebody fetch the kettle!"

Charity dashed into the aisle, lifted her skirts and ran for the house.

"Oh for heaven's sake," Nellie Davis said. "What's all the fuss?"

She soon found out, as Ebba kept on sneezing.

"Why, the poor thing," said Mr. Davis. "She's likely to sneeze herself to death if she doesn't stop."

"She is not going to sneeze to death, Daddy," Charlotte said. "But the poor girl shouldn't be outside."

"Well! I daresay she's not going to make a very good farmer's wife, now is she?" Nellie sneered.

"Mother, behave yourself!" Charlotte's scolded.

Nellie turned to fire back, saw the look of annoyance on her husband's face and decided to glare at her shoes instead.

Ebba's fit continued. Someone was suddenly at her side, but her eyes were so watery she couldn't tell who it was. A handkerchief was placed in her hand and she took it gratefully and blew her nose. She could hear whispers of sympathy along with a few good-natured chuckles. Thankfully, she couldn't hear Nellie Davis anymore.

"Are you all right?" a woman asked.

"I will be…*achoo!*…in a moment…. *achoo!*… I hope."

"Is there anything I can do to help?"

"There's…*achoo!*…nothing I'm afraid."

"Charity's gone to fetch you a cup of tea," Ma said.

Ebba wiped her eyes, glad they were just as affected as her nose was. It would be harder for everyone to tell that she was crying. "I'm so sorry. I've ruined everything."

"We're still gettin' married, sweetie," Daniel said. "All ya have to say is 'I do.'"

"If she can with all that blowing," Nellie added. Beside her, her husband rumbled in warning.

Ebba tried not to glare at Nellie. Her tone was full of accusation, and for the life of her she could not figure out why the woman would say such things.

"She ain't got no disease, does she?" someone asked from the crowd.

There were sudden murmurs from the men. "Maybe Daniel oughtn't marry her," said another.

"What kind of fool talk is that?" Benjamin said and stepped forward as if ready to fight. "My brother's gettin' married today, and no amount of sneezin's gonna stop it!"

"He's right," Daniel agreed. "Go ahead—blow your nose, sweetie, then say 'I do.'"

Ebba gawked at him, looked at the handkerchief, blew her nose, then—*"Achoo!"*

"My my," Nellie said. "Now that went well, didn't it?"

"Nellie, keep out of this!" Leona huffed.

Ebba heard Nellie laugh. It was enough to send her over the edge. She blew her nose again, squared her shoulders, looked the preacher in the eye and managed to yell "I do!" before sneezing again.

Daniel didn't care. He pulled her into his arms and held her tight. "Quick, preacher! Tell me to kiss her!"

"Er…ah…" The preacher took a moment to regain his composure. "By-the-power-vested-in-me-by-Almighty-God-and-the-Washington-Territory-I-now-declare-you-man-and-wife-you-may-kiss-the-bride!"

Ebba sucked in a breath, about to sneeze again, when Daniel reached up and pinched her nose, cutting it short. He then gave her a quick kiss and let her go.

As the cheers began, she stumbled, her sneezing picking up again with a vengeance. Daniel no sooner pulled her against him than Charity came running down the aisle, a cup of tea in her hands. "Quick, drink this!"

Tears were streaming down Ebba's face as she did her best to choke back a sob. But she could still see Nellie with that knowing smirk on her face, while the rest of the townsfolk watched with a combination of sympathy and shock. There were also a few looks of utter disgust, and deep down she knew they weren't because of her sneezing fit. If only she knew what *did* cause them.

"There now, sweetie," Daniel whispered against her hair. "Drink that tea down."

She took a sip, then another. It was hard to breathe but the hot brew helped. Since her voice would betray her at this point, she didn't say anything. Nor did she protest when Daniel picked her up in his arms and carried her back to the house. A few clapped as they passed while the rest murmured congratulations.

With one exception. Nellie Davis could be heard harrumphing, "Well, we'll see how long this marriage lasts."

Fresh tears stung Ebba's eyes. Why would Nellie say such a thing?

"There now, sweetie," Daniel said as he set her on the bed in her room. *Their* room now, she realized. "Ya'll be all right. I'll have Charity bring up another cup of tea."

Ebba tried to hold the tears back but failed. "I'm so sorry!" she sobbed. "I ruined our wedding!"

Daniel, his arms still around her, chuckled. "Now, I wouldn't say that."

She sniffed and wiped her eyes with the back of one hand. "Well, I certainly would…*achoo!*…oh drat!"

"Ya go ahead and sneeze your pretty little head off if'n ya wanna. I don't mind."

She wiped at her face again. The handkerchief the woman had given her earlier was soaked through. "I mind."

"'Course ya do. You're a woman. Womenfolk are always fussin' about this sort of thing. Menfolk, not so much. We know there's some things that cain't be helped."

Ebba swallowed hard. "Well, it's nice…" She sniffed back more tears. "…to know that you don't mind. But to everyone else, I'm a…ah…*achoo!*" She blew her nose. "A laughingstock!"

Daniel reached up and brushed some hair off her face. "Yer mighty pretty today, did ya know that?"

Ebba's mouth dropped open. "How can you say that?" she asked, her voice cracking. "I'm a mess! A horrible mess!"

"Nah," he said gently and cupped her face with one hand. "Yer my wife." And he just as gently, kissed her.

Miracle of miracles, she didn't sneeze. Instead, she let the sensations that simple kiss evoked engulf her. Warmth crept up her spine as his lips melded against hers. One of his arms locked around her waist, while the hand that cupped her face slid to the back of her neck. He deepened the kiss, and she moaned.

Daniel slowly lifted his face from hers. "There now," he whispered against her lips. "That seems to work."

"Wha?" she managed. She couldn't move—her limbs felt like jelly.

"Ya don't sneeze when I kiss ya," he said matter-of-factly. "I kinda like that."

She closed her eyes, unable to keep them open. "Oh."

Daniel pulled her closer and tucked her head under his chin. "I think I might be what cures ya, sweetie. Ain't that somethin'?"

Ebba felt as if she was about to fall into a deep sleep. That Daniel rubbed his hand up and down her back was part of that, and it felt wonderful.

He kissed her hair. "We're gonna be just fine, ya and me," he whispered before gently pulling away to look at her. "Hello, Mrs. Weaver. How ya feelin'?"

Ebba's mouth moved, but nothing came out.

Daniel cupped her face again, lowered his lips to hers and ran his tongue over them as he tightened his arms again.

Her breathing picked up. Where her ailment had stopped, something had started in its place. What it was, she wasn't sure, but it was definitely gaining momentum. The room was growing hot, as were a few other things, when Daniel's tongue delved into her mouth and began to explore. It was all she could do to stay on the bed. If he hadn't been holding her, she'd slide onto the floor in a heap!

The kiss became more demanding and Ebba didn't know what to do. So she kissed him back—or at least hoped she did. Having never been kissed before, she had to improvise, and she was still in a state of shock besides. Not just because he was kissing her, but because she hadn't sneezed once since he'd started. What if kissing kept her from sneezing? Wait—was that what he'd been talking about a moment ago?

Ebba's eyes sprang open at the thought. But she was careful to not move otherwise as Daniel continued to administer the cure to everything that ailed her.

After an hour of Daniel's miracle elixir—kissing Ebba senseless—the newlywed couple came downstairs. Her face washed and her veil straightened, Ebba strode into the parlor on her husband's arm feeling like a new woman. The man was a miracle. Her sneezing had completely stopped, her eyes were dry, the scratch in her throat was gone. Even her voice was fine. All that from kissing? How was she ever going to explain this?

"Are you feeling better, dear?" Leona asked. "You look better."

"I'm much better, thank you," Ebba said.

"She'll be fine," Daniel informed them. "I took care of her."

Nellie, sitting in a chair near the fireplace, glanced at the ceiling before giving them a knowing look. "I'll just bet you did."

Ebba saw Daniel's eyebrows twitch at the remark, but he remained silent.

"Would you like some supper?" Leona asked Daniel. "Your mother is outside serving everyone. Let me go fetch the two of you a plate, shall I?"

"No, you sit with my wife, Mrs. Riley," Daniel instructed. "I'll go get Ebba something to eat."

"Why, that's very kind of you! Don't mind if I do." Leona took Ebba by the hand and led her to the settee. "Come, dear, sit next to me and we'll make sure that sneezing of yours doesn't get started again."

"Are you going to make her some tea?" someone across the room asked.

Ebba and Daniel both looked to see who it was. A thin young woman stood in the doorway to the hall. She had brown hair and amber eyes, almost like a cat's.

"Hello," Ebba said. "I don't believe we've met."

The woman walked over and held out her hand. "I'm Bernice Johnson. My husband Warren is outside helping with supper."

"Ya mean he's outside helpin' with the pig, don't ya?" Daniel asked.

Bernice smiled. "Yes, he is. It's wonderful too."

"You've already eaten?" Ebba asked in surprise. She glanced at Leona sitting next to her.

"Yes, most of us have. You two were upstairs for… quite a while."

"Hmph," Nellie added.

Ebba did her best to ignore her. "How long were we up there?" she asked Daniel, who could only shrug.

"It doesn't matter, dear," said Leona. "What does is that you're feeling better now."

Daniel was still hovering near the door to the hall-way, as if afraid to leave her. The thought warmed Ebba's heart and she felt herself relax. "All I need now is a bite to eat," she hinted, smiling at him.

"Oh! Right—I'll go fetch that plate." He disappeared in a hurry.

Nellie sat and shook her head in disgust.

"What?" Ebba asked, unable to take it anymore.

Nellie slowly faced her. "What?"

It was all Ebba could do not to roll her eyes. Maybe this wasn't the best time to say anything. "Nothing." She turned her attention back to Bernice. "Was it you that handed me a handkerchief earlier?"

"Yes, it was." Bernice sat in the chair next to Nel-lie's. "I hope it helped."

"More than you know," Ebba said. "I hope I can have it washed for you before you leave tomorrow."

Bernice smiled and shook her head. "Keep it. You can save it as a memento of your wedding day."

Nellie laughed.

Ebba forced herself to stay civil. Thankfully, Leona decided to take it upon herself to deal with Nellie.

"You're taking far too much pleasure in this poor child's misery, Nellie Davis! Just what has gotten into you these days?"

Nellie stood. "A better question is, why hasn't anything gotten through to you, Leona?" She cast a quick glance at Ebba. "Or haven't you heard?"

"Heard what?" Leona shot back, clearly flustered.

Nellie smiled like a cat that had just eaten a canary. "Well, if you haven't heard by now, there's no sense telling you."

Leona stood. "Reverting to your old ways, I see," she muttered, then louder: "Fine, don't tell me—I don't want to know." She turned to Bernice. "Go check on what's keeping Daniel, will you, dear?"

"I'll do it," Nellie volunteered. "Besides, I'm sure he's looking forward to getting his wife to himself again." She left the room without another word.

Ebba let out the breath she'd been holding. "That woman is impossible."

"Don't we know it?" Bernice replied. "And to think she was doing so well, too."

"She was?"

"She's a hard one to get along with, that Nellie," Leona said. "Always has been."

"Maybe she's just having a bad day?" Bernice suggested.

"No, she's got ahold of something, I can tell," said Leona.

Ebba fought against a shudder. That *something* obviously had to do with her. She just wished she knew what.

Chapter Sixteen

"So..." Stanley Oliver, Nowhere's blacksmith, elbowed Daniel in the ribs. "How was she?"

"Stanley!" Lucien Miller, the new banker in town, chastised. "Gentlemen do not ask such things of other gentlemen."

"Heck, Mr. Miller," Stanley said. "Everyone 'round here knows I ain't no gentleman like yerself. And neither's Daniel." He turned to Daniel again. "So?"

Daniel's face twisted in confusion. "What in Sam Hill are ya talkin' 'bout, Stanley?"

Stanley's eyes darted around before he leaned toward him. "Now doggone it, Daniel, ya gotta tell me. Yer wife won't care if'n I know. Heck, who knows how many fellers she's been with afore now."

Daniel almost dropped the plate in his hand. "*What* did you say?"

"YaknowhatImean. Truth is, I cain't hardly believe ya married her. I never would. Did ya feel sorry for her or somethin'?"

Daniel handed the plate to Lucien, who took it without question. "What are ya sayin', Stanley? And choose yer words carefully."

Stanley laughed. "C'mon, Danny boy—ain't a man in town that ain't heard about yer wife!"

Lucien cleared his throat. Daniel spun on him. "What have they heard?"

"I have heard nothing worth taking stock in, Mr. Weaver."

He spun back to Stanley, grabbed him by his shirt collar and got right in his face. "What have ya heard?" he snarled.

Stanley quickly took stock and saw two of Daniel's brothers within shouting distance. One Weaver was bad enough, but three was a death sentence. "Er...ya know...that she's a...a..."

Daniel gave him a good shake. "A what?"

"Dagnabit it, yer gonna ruin my best shirt!"

"A *what*?" Daniel repeated and shook him again.

Stanley's voice dropped to a whisper. "A whore."

Lucien groaned and shook his head.

Daniel's eyes popped. "What...did...you...say?"

"Ya heard me—heck, it's all over town—" Stanley didn't get to finish—not after Daniel's fist connected squarely with his jaw. The blacksmith hit the ground hard, and didn't even have a chance to get his hands up before Daniel landed on him and let his fists fly.

Lucien, having been in town long enough to witness Weavers in action (and hear tales of earlier exploits), wisely backed away. As Daniel pummeled away and Stanley began to return fire, he studied the fried chicken on the plate, took a bite and continued to watch, careful not to get his suit dusty. He didn't want to have to clean it.

"What in tarnation's goin' on here?" Arlan roared as he came up beside him.

Lucien swallowed. "Mr. Oliver suggested that Daniel's new bride has an unsavory past. Your brother... took umbrage."

"Well, I don't rightly know what an umberge is, but I figger it cain't be good," Arlan replied. "If it was any other day, I'd let 'em have at it, but Ma won't take kindly to Daniel ruinin' his good clothes." He stepped forward, grabbed Daniel by the shirt collar and yanked him to his feet. Daniel was spitting mad, his arms still swinging, but Arlan shoved him to the side, grabbed Stanley in the same manner and none too gently hauled him up as well. "What's the matter with ya two idjits? Fightin' durin' a weddin' supper?!"

"He called my wife a whore," Daniel said through clenched teeth.

Arlan's eyes narrowed to slits. "He did *what*?"

Stanley's, on the other hand, turned to platters. "Uh-oh..."

Arlan's fist connected with Stanley's jaw, and he dropped like a stone. That done, Arlan returned his attention to Daniel. "Now what started all this?"

"It's like I said! That low-down varmint Stanley called Ebba a whore!"

Arlan glanced at Lucien who nodded. "What the... why in tarnation would he do such a thing?"

Lucien took another bite of chicken, turned and

began to edge away, but was stopped forcibly by Arlan's hand on his collar. "Not so fast. Tell me what ya know."

The young banker sighed and turned around, cringing against any potential fists. "It's a rumor around town, Arlan. I don't know where it started—and frankly, I didn't believe a word of it. Just for the record."

Arlan studied him. Lucien Miller was new in town—he'd arrived the previous autumn, a handsome single man with dark hair and grey eyes. Him being a banker made him suspect to the Weavers, who'd never believed in leaving their money in somebody else's keeping. But he had a reputation for being honest as the day was long. "A rumor, huh?"

"I'm afraid so. I'm sure it's without any basis in fact—"

"So am I!" Daniel declared. "And I'll lick anyone that says otherwise!"

"Calm down, Daniel—I'm sure it ain't the case. But I'd hate for Ebba to have to hear any of this. Might hurt her feelings." Arlan put his hands on his hips as Stanley moaned, and looked around at the crowd that had gathered. "Anyone else heard someone spreadin' dirt about my sister-in-law's virtue?"

Everyone from Nowhere mumbled something in the affirmative.

"Well, I'm tellin' ya right now it ain't true, and anyone who says it is'll answer to me and my brothers. And when I find out who started it, that feller's gonna wish he hain't."

Stanley started trying to sit up.

"Stay down, Stanley," Arlan warned. "I won't hit ya again, but Daniel might."

"Daniel *will*," Daniel corrected.

Stanley lay down again.

"All right," Arlan declared. "Show's over. Y'all go back to whatever you were doin'. And someone get the doc to patch up Stanley—and make sure he don't open his mouth again."

Daniel glared at his brother. "I still wanna hit him."

"I think you've done enough for one day. It's a good thing Ma went into the house or ya'd be gettin' a lickin' of yer own. Leave him be and go do…whatever ya were you doin' out here."

"Fetchin' Ebba a plate."

Lucien looked guiltily at the plate in his hand. "Oh dear…"

Daniel waved him off. "Don't worry none, Luce. I'll fix her another."

Lucien smiled. "Thank you, Daniel. Most generous of you." He nodded farewell and walked away. Arlan gave his brother one last warning glare and did the same.

Daniel sighed, took a few steps after him, then quickly glanced around before kicking Stanley Oliver in the ribs. Whistling, he stuck his hands in his pockets and went to fetch his bride some food.

Ebba was content to stay indoors for now. She knew if she stayed outside for too long, her sneezing would start again and…well, she certainly didn't mind Ma's cures (or Daniel's cure, for that matter), but it was better not to deal with the malady at all. Even aside from the physical toll, there was also her embarrassment to think of.

How she would survive being a farmer's wife was beyond her at this point—her wedding ceremony was proof enough of that. If deep kisses, whiskey and chamomile tea were her only solace, she might have a really fun time, but she wasn't going to be much help to the rest of the Weavers. She grimaced at the thought and sliced up another pie.

"Ebba!" Ma said as she entered the kitchen. "What are you doing that for? You're not supposed to be working—you're the bride!"

Ebba shrugged. "I just needed something to do," she said lamely.

"Nonsense, you have plenty to do—being with your husband, mingling with your guests..."

"Ma," Ebba sighed, "we both know they're your guests, not mine. If I go outside I'm going to have another sneezing fit and I just don't need that. Neither does anyone else, for that matter."

Ma took the knife from her hand, gently pushed her out of the way and finished slicing the pie. "We'll find a remedy that works, mark my words. You might suffer a little now, but you won't later."

Ebba smiled half-heartedly. "How can you be so sure?"

"We won't know unless we keep trying, now will we?" Ma shoved the sliced pie toward Ebba and started on another. "Take that into the parlor and see if anyone wants another piece."

"You're changing the subject on purpose," Ebba pointed out.

"I'm doing nothing of the kind," Ma said innocently. "I think Charlotte and Matthew might like a slice. If Bernice Johnson is in there with them, why don't you talk with them? You're all about the same age. Make some friends, for Heaven's sake."

"What good does it do to make friends when I'll never see them again?" Ebba said before she could stop herself.

Ma quit her slicing, her mouth half open. "What are you talking about? You're not planning to…to run away, are you?"

"No, of course not. I just… I…oh, I don't know."

Ma sighed and put down the knife. "Ebba, I know that maybe Daniel and the rest of us weren't what you had in mind, but know that we love you already and you're part of this family now. And I'll tell you one thing—there is nothing, I mean *nothing*, that's ever going to change that. Do you understand?"

A sudden pang of…well, something, struck Ebba in the heart. It didn't hurt, yet it didn't make her feel any better either. She wasn't quite sure what it was other than perhaps understanding. "Thank you, Ma. I needed to hear that." She took the pie and left the kitchen.

In the parlor Matthew and Charlotte sat on the settee listening to Warren Johnson tell a story. He and Bernice occupied the chairs near the fireplace. "… And that's when Grandpa thought he might get himself a mail-order bride!"

"You mean your grandfather is sending away for a bride?" Charlotte asked in shock. "At his age?"

"What do you mean, 'his age'?" Matthew asked. "Sheriff Hughes and Aunt Mary are probably going to be married soon. Why not Old Man Johnson?"

"I don't know," she said. "It just seems as though he'd be bringing in another person for Bernice and Warren to take care of."

"I don't mind," Bernice said. "And Grandpa gets around fine for his age. He works just as hard as Warren every day. Another pair of hands around the house would be fine with me."

"Besides, his new bride might not be as old," Warren added. "Younger women do marry older men sometimes."

Ebba cleared her throat. "Excuse me, but would any of you like a slice of pie?"

"Don't mind if I do," Matthew said and stood. He went to a sideboard where a stack of plates had been placed, took five and handed them out. When he got to Ebba, he gave her one and took the pie. "I'll serve."

Ebba handed him the pie and the server. "Why, thank you."

Matthew nodded and began to dole out the pie. "What's your opinion, Ebba?" he asked.

"Of what?"

"Ma Weaver and Sheriff Hughes getting married."

Ebba took a step back. "I don't think that's any of our business, do you?"

"She's my aunt—that makes it a little bit my business."

Ebba wasn't sure what to say. How much did they know? "I don't think I'm the one you should be asking. You should talk to Ma or Sheriff Hughes."

"Harlan has made his intentions quite clear to some of the men. But my question is, what do *you* think of them marrying each other?"

"Are you asking this because of their age?"

"Yes. I'm curious. If Old Man Johnson can get a mail-order bride, then why can't a man like Harlan, or say, Hank, who owns the restaurant in town, get hitched as well?"

Ebba was beginning to get flustered. "Why are you asking me this?"

He set the pie plate on the sideboard. "Because of a belief I have."

Everyone in the room stared at him. "Matthew, whatever are you talking about?" Charlotte asked.

Matthew squared his shoulders. "I believe that no one in this world should be alone if they don't want to be. Even the Good Book says 'it is not good for man to be alone.' There must be a reason for that, don't you think?"

"Are you saying that people should try their best not to be alone? I mean, remain single? That everyone should get married?" Ebba asked.

"Not necessarily marriage. I'm saying that people need people, whether they marry or are simply with family and friends. But if two people love each other, they shouldn't let minor problems get in the way of their happiness."

Ebba bit her lower lip. He had to be talking about her

and the sneezing fit she had earlier. What else could it be? "What if two people love each other but one of them has something that drives the other person crazy?"

Matthew retook his seat. "If they love each other, they'll find a way. Lord knows Charlotte and I have had our differences over the years, and we've had to learn to adjust to each other."

Ebba watched sadness flash across Charlotte's face. "I see. So if two people aren't in love yet and have something they have to deal with…" *Oh, for Heaven's sake,* she thought. *Ask the real question.* "All right. What if Daniel and his family can't put up with my constant sneezing?!"

Matthew didn't turn a hair. "He married you, didn't he? Once one of my cousins makes a vow, trust me, they don't break it."

"Why are you worried about such a thing?" Bernice asked her.

Ebba glanced at each of them before she spoke. "I guess…it's because I don't really know them yet." *Or maybe I just don't trust him yet,* she added silently. She still had to talk to him about all the things he hadn't told her. Who knew what else she'd discover? Is that why everyone gave her such funny looks in town, or today at the wedding? Is that what had put the bee in Nellie Davis's bonnet? And if not that, then what?

And then there was her sneezing and sniffling on top of that…well, there was a lot that needed to be worked out, anyone could see.

"Ebba," Bernice said. "Won't you sit with us and enjoy this pie?"

Ebba looked down at her plate and sure enough, Matthew had served her a slice. In all her turmoil, she hadn't even registered it. Whereas Daniel still hadn't returned with the promised plate of food for her. One more question she needed to ask. But not right now—she didn't have the will for it. "Yes…thank you," she said as she sat.

Chapter Seventeen

"I'm sorry it took me so long to fetch ya a plate, Ebba," Daniel said for the fifth time. The wedding celebration was over by now. The guests were camped out around the farmhouse or the barn or Arlan and Samijo's place.

"Daniel, you've apologized enough. It's all right—that was hours ago." Ebba still didn't know why it had taken so long, and that annoyed her. But not as much as the constant apologizing.

"But I wanna explain myself. Especially now."

"Then explain. But do stop saying you're sorry." Ebba looked out the bedroom window at the campfires some of the guests had built. She wished she could be out there sitting next to one. Warren and Bernice were laughing with Charlotte and Matthew while Mr. and Mrs. Davis sat quietly nearby.

Daniel peeked over her shoulder and watched as well. "They look cozy, don't they?"

"Yes," she said, unable to keep the envy out of her voice.

"Ebba," he began again. "Ya know what tonight is?"

She swallowed hard. "Yes, Daniel, I know."

He put his hands on her shoulders and turned her to face him. "Ya don't sound too happy about it."

She closed her eyes and sighed. "I…have a lot on my mind."

"Am I one of them thoughts?"

She opened her eyes and met his. "Yes." In one way or another, he was all of them.

His eyes pooled with worry. "If'n I am, how come ya don't look happy? Ya married me."

"I know and…maybe now is not the time, but…"

"But what? What do ya mean?"

Oh, hang it all, just say *it!* she scolded herself. "We need to talk about some things."

He let his hands fall from her. "Um…ya mean about…our weddin' night?"

She drew in a breath. "In a way."

His eyes widened. "What way?"

She squared her shoulders. "There have been a lot of things you haven't been telling me. Things you should have."

"Like what?"

"Like you having over twenty relatives living here."

"Well, um… I didn't think it was that important."

Ebba resisted the urge to raise her voice. "It's very important. Or how you expect me to become a teacher for all the children."

He shrugged. "Well, yeah, but what's that got to do with our weddin' night?"

"Why didn't you tell me? Why didn't you say anything in your letters?"

"Because I didn't need to."

"What do you mean, you didn't need to?" she said in shock. "Didn't you think I'd need to know that? There are fifteen children on this farm!"

"Only if'n ya count the babies," he added. "Heck, Rufi don't hardly count at all."

"Well, babies don't stay babies, or didn't you know that?" She turned back toward the window. "You should have mentioned in your letters what you expected of me."

"But I didn't say anything in my letters…"

She spun back. "That's my point! Did it ever occur to you that becoming a…a…schoolmarm for your nieces and nephews is a really big job? What if I was incapable of such a task?"

"Ya can read and write, can't ya?"

"Of course!"

He cocked his head to one side. "Don't tell me ya don't know yer numbers?"

Ebba rolled her eyes. "Yes, I know my numbers! But it takes a lot more than that to be a teacher. And even if it didn't, you still didn't tell me—not in your letters, not when I arrived, not until now when I called you on it! I had to find out from Rufi!"

"Well…uh…"

She narrowed her eyes at him. "What else haven't you told me?"

Daniel took a step back and laughed nervously. "Is

that what this is about? Ya think I'm holdin' some-thin' out on ya?"

"You certainly have been so far," she snapped. "Holding out on a lot of things."

Daniel looked around as if for help. Finding none, he took a deep breath and let it out slowly. "Darlin', how could I have told ya in them letters about teachin' when the idea done hit me only after ya got here?"

Ebba went still. "What?"

"Ya heard me. I didn't get the idea 'til I saw ya sneezin' and strugglin' so hard to breathe the first day. It figgered ya couldn't work outside with the rest of us, that ya'd need a job that can be done indoors. With all these younguns 'round here, you becomin' their teacher was perfect. Or...so I thought."

Ebba's brow furrowed in confusion. "But... Rufi said something about my letters..."

"Aw, Rufi's still just a kid—she gets things mixed up. You and me was talking about readin' and writin' in them letters, so I suggested it to Calvin and Bella, and...she musta overheard and got it all crossed. Be-sides, I didn't promise nothin' 'cept that I'd ask ya if ya wanted to give it a try. And we've been so busy with the weddin' that I figgered I should hold off 'til ya got settled in and..."

"... And you weren't going to require it of me?"

"Nah, just offer it and see what ya thought." He sighed and took her in his arms. "I'm sorry if'n I didn't make myself clear. I guess I messed it up real thorough."

She leaned into him. The warmth of his body felt good. "I'm sorry too. I...shouldn't have assumed. And

I shouldn't have snapped at you the way I did. It's just frustrating when you don't know what's coming."

Daniel kissed the top of her head. "I understand. Ain't nothin' To be sorry for, sweetie. Ma says a husband and wife are gonna have buckets of misunderstandin's durin' a marriage. We just gotta figger out how to not fill them buckets so fast."

Ebba smiled. "Your mother is a very wise woman."

"Don't I know it. And now I know to tell ya more stuff so ya don't get caught unawares."

She shyly lifted her arms and put them around his waist. "I'd appreciate that, thank you."

He looked at her. "Well, that's one bucket emptied."

She smiled as she gazed into his eyes. "Yes, it is."

His eyes darted to her lips and, before she knew it, she was lost in his kiss. His hands roamed her back as it deepened, pulling a moan from her.

He gently broke the kiss. "I like it when you make that sound," he whispered against her lips. "I want to hear ya do it again."

Ebba shook her head. "I'm not so sure…"

Daniel smiled. "I'm sure, though." He kissed her again.

Ebba moaned again. Pretty soon, she was as sure as he was. And that surety carried them into the rest of the night.

When Ebba awoke the next morning, Daniel was already gone. She sat up, realized she hadn't a stitch of clothing on and yanked the blankets up to her neck. The previous night came back in a rush and she giggled in delight. She and Daniel were now truly husband and wife. They'd both been clumsy at first, but nature has a way of making the clumsiest dancer graceful under its tutelage. And they had danced well into the night.

She was surprised she was even up…but then, what time was it? Wrapping a blanket around herself, she went to the window and found the sun high in the sky, though not at its peak. Well, at least it wasn't noon yet. She went to the washstand and quickly got ready for the rest of her day.

She spied her wedding dress draped over a chair and smiled at the memory of Daniel carefully removing it…she shook herself. Best not to think of such things now—she had work to do. She hoped she wasn't too late to help with lunch.

Downstairs, she found Charity in the kitchen making sandwiches. "Good morning, Ebba," she greeted her with a smile. "Sleep well?"

Ebba blushed bright pink.

"I see you did. Good. Daniel's out helping some of the others break camp. I'm afraid the two of you missed breakfast."

Ebba, for lack of a better idea, shrugged.

Charity laughed. "You don't have to say anything. There's a stack of flapjacks in the warming oven. That is, if your husband left you any."

Ebba went to the warming oven and took out the plate. "Thank you for saving us some." She folded one and was about to take a bite when it registered what Charity was doing. "Wait—is it lunchtime already?"

"Not quite, but close. I'm making these for the folks

leaving in a bit so they can eat on the road. They'll stay at the Gundersons' tonight before they head on to Nowhere. No one got up too early today."

"Is that supposed to make me feel better?"

"No, that's to let you know everyone had a good time at your wedding." She went to Ebba and gave her a hug. "Myself included. Welcome to the family."

Tears welled in Ebba's eyes. She hadn't realized until that moment that now she had a family again. A huge one! "Thank you, Charity."

Charity smiled as she went back to the worktable. "Do you want to help me finish these?" she asked as she swept a hand over the sandwiches.

"Certainly." They made a dozen more, wrapped them, put them into baskets and took them outside to pass out. Ebba began to tick off the minutes it would take before she began to sneeze. She figured she was good for ten at the most.

She went to the Johnsons' wagon and handed the basket to Bernice. "Here you are—something for the trip."

Bernice smiled and took it from her. "Thank you! I didn't plan for the trip back very well."

"Don't worry, you're not the only one. But Charity made enough sandwiches to feed an army."

"Did you...have a nice night?"

Ebba flushed red. Was it really ladylike to ask such a question? Well, it seemed to be out here. When in Rome... "I did," she whispered.

Bernice glanced at her before she looked away again. "Oh, that's...good."

"Well, I'd better pass the rest of these out," Ebba said and began to turn away.

"I'm sorry."

"For what?"

"For asking something so personal. It's just that… well…"

Ebba faced her and waited. "Well, what?"

"It's nothing."

Ebba didn't push it. She'd come to find out that the folks of Nowhere were a little strange. Perhaps all small towns were like that. She set her other basket down and gave Bernice a hug. "Thank you for coming."

"You're welcome. I hope you and Daniel will be very happy."

"I'm sure we will be." She went off to deliver more sandwiches, passing the rest out to the Rileys and the Davises before heading to the barn to see who was left. A man, a Mr. Oliver if she remembered right, was just coming out. "Would you like something to take on the road with you?" she asked.

Mr. Oliver looked her up and down. "Sure would, little lady. A nice taste of somethin' would suit me just fine."

Ebba smiled and started to reach into her basket, but before she could grab a sandwich, he had her locked in his arms and was dragging her into the barn. "What the mmmph?" The hand he clamped over her mouth was sweaty, dirty and smelled, and his other arm had hers pinned to her sides.

He headed for an empty stall and dragged her into

it. "I've been waitin' for this since I first set eyes on ya! Woo-ee, I bet you're gonna be sweet!"

Ebba, realizing what he was about, kicked and struggled with all her might, but it was no use. The man had the strength of an ox. He threw her onto the straw and was on top of her before she could scream for help.

Mr. Oliver, much to her surprise, did it for her. "YEOWWW!" He leapt off her and spun around, swinging the pitchfork now attached to his derriere with him. A string of curses escaped before he fell to his knees—and then on his face, as a large foot kicked him in the back of the skull.

Ebba looked up. Daniel stood looming over her assailant, his face twisted in anger. He stepped over Mr. Oliver, reached down and took her in his arms. "Ebba, are ya all right?"

She blinked at him a few times before the import of what had just happened sank in. "He…he…was…"

"I know what he was gonna do. And I guarantee ya he won't be thinkin' of doin' anything like it again!"

"What's going on in here?" Sheriff Hughes appeared at the stall door. "What in tarnation happened to him?"

"He was up to no good, Sheriff!" Daniel said. "Ya gotta arrest him!"

"Arrest him? I think I need to get him to a doctor first!"

"The likes of him don't deserve no doctor," Daniel said as he held Ebba tighter. "Get him outta my sight before I stick that pitchfork where I wanted to in the first place!"

Sheriff Hughes studied the scene. "Did he try to…?" His finger wagged between Stanley and Ebba.

"Yes, he did," Ebba sobbed. The emotions were starting to break through her shock.

"I understand." He looked at Ebba. "You okay?"

"I just offered him some sandwiches for the road," she whimpered. "Why would he…"

"Shhh, it's over," Daniel said soothingly, stroking her hair. "He ain't never gonna touch ya again. Not if I can help it."

"That goes double for me," the sheriff agreed. "I'll fetch Spencer. This is a serious situation, Daniel. Spencer *will* have to arrest him."

"Jail's too good for the snake."

"I don't disagree, Daniel, but the law is the law." Sheriff Hughes sighed. "Get your wife back to the house. Spencer and I will handle this."

Daniel nodded. "Ya sure yer all right, sweetie?"

She nodded. The man had wanted to rape her, but why? And in broad daylight, *in the barn?* "I don't understand…what was he thinking?"

"He wasn't." Daniel led her out of the stall, exchanging a quick look with Sheriff Hughes as he did. That convinced Ebba they knew exactly what Mr. Oliver was thinking. But wouldn't anyone tell her?

Ebba sat at the kitchen table, a hot cup of tea in her hands. "I didn't do or say anything other than offer the man a sandwich. He grabbed me and pulled me into the barn so fast, I didn't have time to think."

Clayton and Spencer sat across the table from her. "And he didn't say anything?"

Ebba cringed. "He said…" She swallowed back the bile in her throat. "…he said that he'd been waiting for *it* since he'd first laid eyes on me." She glanced at Daniel standing next to her, and noticed his hands were balled into fists.

"Thank you, Ebba." Spencer waved the other men in the room toward the kitchen's back door. "We'll discuss this outside and let you be."

"Are ya gonna be all right if'n I go outside too?" Daniel asked her.

"Yes, of course," she said. Daniel nodded and headed out after the others.

"Would you like some more tea?"

Ebba jumped in her chair. "Oh, Charity! I'm sorry—yes, please."

Charity took the cup from her and went to refill it. "I'm sorry about what happened to you. I'm also glad that nothing else happened."

Ebba shuddered at the thought. Thank the Lord Daniel had come along when he did. "I just don't understand men like that. How they can…"

"I know." Charity set Ebba's teacup back in its saucer. "I've…been through something similar."

Ebba turned in her chair to face her. "You have?"

Charity nodded. "It was a horrible ordeal, but the good Lord brought blessing out of it."

Ebba gaped at her. "What good can come out of something so horrible?"

Charity glanced at the ceiling. "My son."

Ebba could only stare. "Sebastian?!"

"Yes."

Ebba's hand flew to her mouth "Oh Charity… I had no idea…"

"No one but the family knows."

"I'm so sorry."

"Don't be. Benjamin and I have a beautiful son that we're raising. In fact, if it weren't for Benjamin and this family I don't know what I would have done."

Ebba continued to stare. "I… I can't imagine…"

"And you don't have to." Charity took a chair and sat. "Be glad Stanley Oliver didn't get the chance. It would have caused a horrible chain of events…"

"What do you mean?"

Charity looked her in the eye. "Daniel and his brothers *would* have killed him."

Ebba's eyes bulged. "No!"

"Sheriff Riley will see that Stanley Oliver is dealt with. I just can't get over that he would do such a thing with so many people around…"

"I can."

Both women turned to see Nellie Davis standing in the doorway. "What do you mean?" Charity asked. "What he tried to do is inexcusable."

"That would depend on who he was doing it with, I suppose." Nellie turned her attention on Ebba. "I told you I wouldn't see this family harmed. Now look what you've done."

Charity jumped to her feet. "Mrs. Davis, have you no decency? How dare you talk to her like that! Ebba has done nothing wrong!"

Nellie eyed both of them coolly. "Hasn't she?" Without explanation, she marched out the back door.

Ebba gripped the edge of the table. "I don't understand that woman! She keeps throwing those barbs at me, and I don't know why! What did I ever do to her?"

"Never mind her—she's always been that way." Charity reached out and patted Ebba on shoulder.

The door opened before Ebba could reply, and Spencer and Clayton Riley returned to the kitchen, followed by Daniel. "The judge will be passing through town next week, Mrs. Weaver," Spencer told her. "I'd like you and Daniel to come to town and testify."

"Testify?" Ebba said weakly.

"Yes," Spencer said. "I've arrested Stanley Oliver for attempted rape."

Ebba sank in her chair. How had her life taken such a turn in only a few hours?

"It's all right, sweetie," Daniel said as he stood behind her and put his hands on her shoulders. "I'll be right there with ya."

"But he didn't actually…" Ebba started to say.

"But he tried," said Clayton. "That's against the law too."

"And we want to make sure he doesn't try again," Spencer added.

Ebba put her face in her hands. "Oh dear…"

Daniel bent down and hugged her. "It's gonna be okay, honey, you'll see. But that man's gotta be punished. We cain't let him get away with somethin' like this."

"The Davises just left," Ma said as she entered the

kitchen with Sheriff Hughes. "I must say that Nellie was acting..." Ma stopped when she saw the looks on everyone's faces. "What's going on?"

"Harlan, did you tell her?" Clayton asked.

"I was about to. Not everyone knows."

"Nellie does," Charity said flatly.

"Why doesn't that surprise me?" Spencer said, glancing at Clayton.

"Tell me what?" Ma asked sharply.

"Ma," Daniel said softly, "Stanley Oliver done took Ebba into the barn and...tried to have his way with her."

"WHAT?!"

Harlan was immediately at her side. "Calm down there. Daniel made sure the varmint didn't do nothing. Ebba just got a little shook up is all. Isn't that right, Ebba?"

Ebba nodded, but couldn't look Ma in the eye. She suddenly remembered the weight of Stanley's body on top of hers and cringed.

Daniel helped her up and held her in his arms. "There now, sweetie, it's all right," he cooed.

Ma waved Harlan off. "On my farm? In my barn? A man tried to...dagnabit!" She turned this way and that, her face locked in helpless rage.

"Mary, Ebba's all right," Harlan said.

Ma spun on him, stopped, then shut her eyes tight as if that would make it all go away.

"Ma," Daniel said. "Sheriff Riley's gonna see to it the low-down snake gets what's comin' To him. Everythin's gonna be all right."

Ma opened her eyes and met Harlan's, her lower jaw trembling. "Yes."

Harlan glanced around the room, then back to Mary. "Yes what?"

"Yes, Harlan, I'll marry you."

Harlan took a step back as everyone else stared in shock. "Wha?"

Ma's eyes filled with tears. "I can't go through something like this by myself, Harlan." She looked at Ebba and Daniel. "I can't be all I need to be for these younguns alone."

"Ma…" Charity began. Ebba looked at her and shook her head. Charity took the cue and went silent.

"Mary," Harlan began, "I understand this is a shock, but don't let this situation decide for you. I want you to want to marry me because you…"

"I do!"

"…love me," he finished weakly.

She nodded, tears in her eyes. "I do," she repeated. "I do love you. Now stand here by my side and help me get through this."

Harlan took her in his arms and held her tight. "I'm here for you, Mary. I'm not going anywhere."

Ebba looked into Daniel's eyes, smiled, then glanced at Charity. "Blessings out of tragedy?"

Charity smiled back. "Exactly."

Chapter Eighteen

Over the next couple of weeks the Weaver clan developed a new routine. Chaotic breakfasts were followed by Bella's siblings gathering in the main farmhouse parlor for lessons with Ebba. After giving it some thought, she'd told Calvin, Bella and Daniel that she'd be willing to be their teacher—on a provisional basis. "We'll see how it goes" were her exact words.

And the first thing she'd taught them was that no pranks would be tolerated. A small frog turning up in her teacup seemed hilarious to the kids…until Ebba told Ma and Ma declared there would be no pie for any of them at lunchtime. The snails in Ebba's apron pocket resulted in Gabby (the perpetrator) having to scrub the porch steps. And when Alfonso and Leo let loose in the house the bunny they'd caught that morning, they were the ones who had to catch it again—while everyone else got to have some of Charity's fudge brownies.

By the end of the second week, all seven were giving her their utmost attention and were so well behaved that Bella went out of her way to praise Ebba's discipline. And they hadn't even tried to tie her to anything. At least not yet.

But the best part of Ebba's new life was her time with Daniel. They too had developed a routine, and no frogs or snails were involved. Bunnies, on the other hand, might show some resemblance. Ebba wondered if she'd be with child before long at that rate.

"Happy?" she asked Daniel one evening as they sat on the porch swing, each with a cup of tea in their hands.

"Sure am. You?"

"Yes. And...thank you."

"For what, sweetie?"

"For coming up with the idea that I teach the children. Between my time indoors and Ma's teas, I'm not sneezing half as much as I used to."

"I still think it's the kissin'."

"Kissing?" she said in shock. "What does kissing have to do with anything?"

"Remember when I kissed ya on our weddin' day and it made yer sneezin' stop?"

Ebba had to think a moment. "Oh yes, you're right."

Daniel smiled and put an arm around her. "I try to be."

She smiled back and studied his face a moment. He was so handsome and strong, yet so tender. "I think I feel a sneeze coming on now," she teased.

"Do ya? Well now, we can't have that, can we?" He leaned toward her for a kiss.

"Daniel!"

They pulled back to see Tom Turner bring his horse to a skidding stop. Daniel stood, spilling his tea. "What is it?"

"Judge is in town," the deputy declared. "We're gonna need Ebba to come testify against Stanley for what he done."

Ebba stood, her hand at her chest. "Oh dear…do I have to?"

Daniel put his arm around her. "If'n we want to make sure he don't do it to no one else, then yeah."

She nodded. "I understand. It's just… I'm not looking forward to it."

Daniel kissed her tenderly. "I'll be right there with ya the whole time, ya hear?"

She nodded again, but said nothing.

Daniel turned to the deputy. "Ya hungry, Tom? There's some stew left."

"Much obliged, Danny boy." Tom tied his horse to the hitching post in front of the house, took the porch steps two at a time and went inside.

"He certainly makes himself at home," Ebba remarked.

"He should—he's spent enough time with us over the years. That man tells the best yarns of anyone I know. Tarnation, I'm gonna miss him when he's gone."

"Gone?"

"Ain't ya heard? Now that Harlan's gonna marry Ma, Tom's gonna be the new sheriff in Clear Creek."

"He's leaving Nowhere?"

"'Fraid so. Ma wants to organize a party for Tom

and Rose 'fore they make the move. Harlan's asked Tom to be his best man at their weddin'."

"She's almost done with her wedding dress. I'm sure she'll finish it tomorrow."

"Looks like we'll be headin' to Nowhere for more than just a weddin' in a day or two. I just hope Ma ain't upset we have to deal with bein' in court at the same time."

"What if we have to be away longer than a few days?" she asked.

He pulled her down onto the swing with him. "Then we deal with it. The rest of the family don't need to be there 'less they're witnesses. I'm the one that came lookin' for ya and found that no-good Stanley…" He took a breath. "I just get so mad thinkin' 'bout it, I wanna hit somethin'!"

"Why were you looking for me right then?" she asked. She'd never thought to ask until now…probably because she was too busy trying to forget the whole thing.

"A gut feelin'."

Her mouth slowly fell open. "You mean…that's it? You went into the barn because of a feeling?"

"Well, it's the same feelin' I get when one of my brothers is in trouble."

Ebba sat up straight and stared at him. "You knew I was in trouble…"

"No. But my gut did. Either that or the good Lord directed my steps right to ya. Gotta be one of the two."

She smiled. The Weaver men were all big and

strong, but with a childlike innocence that couldn't be denied. "I think it was a little of both."

"Most likely," he agreed, pulling her closer. "Ya sure yer ready for this?"

"No. But I'll do what I have to do. What if the judge only holds a hearing?"

"I'm thinking this'll have a jury and everythin'. Everyone in town knows Stanley—they rely on him to shoe their horses and fix stuff for 'em. For the most part he's well respected, and some folks in town might side with him. I respected him too, 'til he called you a..." He snapped his mouth shut.

"Called me a what?" she asked, her head cocked to one side.

"Nothin'."

"Daniel...no more hiding things from me. What did he... Daniel?"

Daniel had removed his arm from around her and was standing up. "Oh my..."

Ebba was alarmed by the blank look on his face. "Daniel, what's wrong?"

"That's it. That's why he thought he could... dagnabit! Why didn't I think of that before?"

"Think of what?"

He sat down again and turned to her. "Ebba darlin', I didn't want to tell ya 'bout this, but there ain't no help for it now."

"Help for what? Daniel, you're talking in riddles."

He sighed heavily. "There's a rumor in town that... well... I dunno how it got started exactly, but..."

Ebba put her hands on her hips. "But what?"

Daniel swallowed hard. "There's folks in town that were sayin' you were a…" He swallowed again. "…a whore."

"What!?" she yelped. "Are you serious? Who on Earth would start such a…oh. Ohhhh…" She fell silent as her eyes narrowed.

Daniel leaned toward her. "Ebba, ya okay?"

"Nellie Davis," she said through gritted teeth.

Daniel was confused. "Nellie Davis? What's she got to do with anythin'?"

"Possibly everything. So that's why she was treating me so awfully! And maybe why everyone else was, if she's the gossiping type."

"She is," Daniel said sourly.

"But why would Mrs. Davis think I'm a…a…you know."

"I don't like sayin' it any more'n ya do, sweetie. And I'm afraid I ain't got no answer for ya. Unless she's just tryin' to stir up trouble like she used to."

Ebba fell back onto the swing. "Why? Why would she do such a thing?"

Daniel shrugged. "She's always been that way. Charlotte was too for a while, 'til she realized no one wanted to marry a girl like that and shaped up. She changed, married cousin Matty, and she's been a peach ever since."

"But why me?"

"I cain't say, sweetie."

Ebba sighed. "I'm sorry. I never meant to cause the family any trouble."

"Ya didn't cause no trouble. Nellie did if'n she

started that rumor. Stanley did, and now he's gonna have to suffer for it. But ya didn't cause nothin' but my happiness." He drew her close and kissed her hair.

Ebba smiled and snuggled against him. "But what about Nellie? What's to keep her from doing something like this again?"

Daniel rubbed her back absently. "Ya know…that's a real good question."

Two days later, in Nowhere…

Judge Henry Whipple was a bear of a man who didn't tolerate any nonsense in his courtroom. Or in this case, Hank's restaurant, as Nowhere didn't have a courthouse and everyone thought the meetinghouse would be too large for the proceedings.

They were wrong about that. Hank's was stuffed to the rafters with people, half of which were there to defend Stanley's character. The other half were waiting to see if he'd survive the proceedings, considering all the Weaver men were present. If there was one thing that particular half liked, it was a good old-fashioned brawl.

Hank had shoved a couple of tables together at one end of the restaurant for the judge to use and placed the others against the walls. The chairs set up in the middle of the room were already taken, so the rest of the townsfolk leaned against or sat on the tables, much to Hank's dismay.

The Weavers were the last to arrive and had to stand where they could. There wasn't room for all of them, of course, so only Ma, Harlan, Benjamin, Calvin, Daniel and Ebba were able to squeeze in. The rest of the women and the children had to wait outside with everyone else unable to claim a space. Arlan was nowhere in evidence.

Ma and Harlan were dressed in their Sunday best as they were hoping to get married afterwards. All Ma would have to do is change into her wedding dress. Harlan would already be in his wedding clothes.

Harlan looked at his future bride and smiled. Ma's hat kept sliding off to one side of her head, making it hard for her to see what was happening. "Where's the judge?" she asked. "I don't see him."

"My guess is that there's the new judge sittin' behind them tables, Ma," Benjamin said.

"What? What happened to Judge Houston?" she asked. "He's been coming through here for years."

The brothers exchanged glances. "Don't rightly know, Ma," Calvin said.

Ma craned her neck to see. Not an easy thing to do at her height. "I wish some of these people would move out of the way."

A sudden rapping on a tabletop caught everyone's attention. All faced forward and noted Judge Whipple's scowl. "This court is now in session," he bellowed, and then waved Spencer Riley toward him. "Let's make this quick, Sheriff. I got me a bellyache."

A few folks chuckled at the remark. The judge picked up his gavel and rapped it on the table again, which made Hank cringe. "I'll have order in this court if you don't mind." He looked at Spencer again. "What have we got?"

Spencer nodded to Tom Turner who marched a handcuffed Stanley Oliver through the crowd to where the judge sat. "This is the accused, Your Honor," Spencer said. "Mr. Stanley Oliver was caught in the act of attempting to defile a young lady."

Judge Whipple's face twisted up in disbelief. "Defile? You mean he tried to rape her?" A few women in the crowd swooned at the word and almost fell out of their chairs. He rapped his gavel on the table again. "If you women can't take this sort of thing, then get out! This is a courtroom, not a quilting bee!" The women quickly straightened up and sat still.

The judge rolled his eyes and shook his head, then looked Stanley over. "How long have you lived here, son?"

"A little over a year, Your Honor, sir," Stanley stated as his eyes darted around the room.

Judge Whipple kept looking him up and down. "Uh-huh." He looked over the crowd before his eyes fell on Spencer again. "And where's his accuser?"

"Right here, Your Honor!" Ma cried from the back of the room. She, Harlan and her sons shoved their way through the crowd, with Ebba in the middle. When they reached the table Ma sighed in relief. "Whew, made it."

The judge seemed confused. He looked at Stanley, at Ma, back again. "Son, you attacked this poor old woman?"

Spencer's jaw tightened in an effort not to laugh. "Mrs. Weaver is not Mr. Oliver's accuser, Your Honor."

Judge Whipple glanced at a paper on the desk. "Says here she is."

"I'm not the Mrs. Weaver he attacked," Ma said as she maneuvered Ebba forward. "She is!"

The judge nodded. "I see. You want to tell me what happened, little lady?"

"Well," Ebba said as she wrung her hands in front of her. "I was handing sandwiches out to…"

The judge belched long and loud, cutting her off. He struck his chest a few times with his fist. "Pardon me. Indigestion." He glared at Hank, who shrank back into the crowd.

"Oh, I'm terribly sorry," Ebba said apologetically.

"You and me both. You were saying?"

She swallowed hard and tried again. "I was handing out the sandwiches and ran into this man here near the barn on the Weaver property."

The judge struck his chest several more times and cleared his throat, his face turning red. "The accused has a name, miss. Use it."

"Yes, Your Honor. Mr. Oliver was coming out of the barn when I offered him a sandwich."

"That ain't all she offered him!" came a shout from the crowd.

The judge brought the gavel down hard upon the table. "Order!" He looked at Ebba. "And?"

"He grabbed me and pulled me into the barn."

"Didn't you think to scream or something?" the judge asked and belched. "Pardon me."

Ebba and everyone else within a few feet of the man wrinkled their noses. Whatever Hank fed him earlier obviously had a lot of onions in it. "I couldn't, sir. He put a hand over my mouth."

The judge eyed Stanley disapprovingly. "Did he?"

Stanley blanched. "I demand a lawyer!"

"There are no lawyers around these parts, boy," the judge said. "I'm all you've got—deal with it."

Stanley's jaw tightened but he said nothing. The judge nodded in satisfaction at the silence and turned back to Ebba. "Then what happened?"

"Well…" she said, wringing her hands once more. "He dragged me into a stall, threw me on the ground and pinned me there."

Several women swooned again, one of which managed to carefully fall onto the floor.

Judge Whipple rolled his eyes and groaned. "Somebody get them out of here! A man's liable to trip over one of 'em!" He turned back to Ebba. "Then what?"

Ebba was momentarily distracted by the fainting women's husbands ushering them through the crowd and out the door. The one who'd hit the floor had the audacity to pretend she was out cold, but Ebba caught her peeking at the crowd as she was dragged away. "Um… I tried to fight him, but he was too strong. And then my husband stabbed him with a pitchfork in the… the, uh…" She reached behind her and pointed at an area below her waist.

"Took a hayfork in the butt, did he?" the judge confirmed. "Is your husband here today, young lady?"

"That'd be me, Yer Honor," Daniel said, raising his hand.

"I'll get to you later, son." Judge Whipple turned to Stanley. "So? What do you have to say for yourself?"

Ebba was still looking around the room. She'd never

been in court before, but knew this was hardly the norm. Why were people being so theatrical about the whole thing? Were they friends of Nellie Davis? And speaking of which, where was Nellie Davis? She didn't appear to be present...

"What she says ain't true!" Stanley cried. "She's just sayin' that 'cause she don't want them Weavers to find out what she really is!" He glared at Daniel. "Not that this'un ain't figgered it out already if'n he's got half a brain—"

The judge banged his gavel again. "Quiet, you! A simple answer will suffice." He grimaced and struck his chest again with his fist. "Dangblasted onions. Oof." He looked at Ebba. "He's calling you a liar, miss. My question is, why would you lie?"

"I wouldn't! He is!"

The judge belched and grimaced again.

"Judge Whipple," Spencer said with concern. "Are you all right, sir?"

The judge waved dismissively at him. "It'll pass. Witnesses?"

"I'm the witness, Yer Honor," Daniel said.

The judge took a few deep breaths and leaned back. "Ah yes, her husband? What did you see?"

"It's just like Ebba said. By the time I got there, he was about to...well, ya know."

"No, I don't know. How am I supposed to know anything if you people won't give me a straight answer?" He belched again. "Land sakes, but I hate this job sometimes. Spell it out, boy!"

Daniel tried again, pointing at Stanley. "I walked in

on this man pinnin' my bride down and tryin' To have his way with her. So I grabbed the first thing I could find in order to stop him!"

"Which was the pitchfork?" the judge asked.

"Which was the pitchfork, yes."

The judge nodded and smiled, then looked at Stanley. "Well, son, it'd be darn deadly difficult to put those tines in your tush unless you were indeed in the position they claim you were."

Stanley's eyes darted furtively about. "She was askin' fer it! Her kind always asks for it. She wanted it too!"

More gasps from the crowd. The judge ignored them. "So now you're claiming that she solicited your affections?"

"'Course she did!" Stanley spat. "What can ya expect from a whore? This whole trial's a farce, I tell ya! No one expects a man to be punished for havin' his way with a common—"

Daniel stepped beside Stanley before he could finish and punched him in the jaw, never once taking his eyes off the judge. "Oops. Sorry, Yer Honor—my fist musta slipped."

Judge Whipple stared in shock at Stanley lying on the floor, then looked up at Daniel again. "Young man, was that really necessary?"

"I believe so, Yer Honor. I'll do whatever it takes to protect my wife, even if it means I have to go to jail, sir."

The judge grumbled to himself for a moment. "Well, under normal circumstances, I'd find you in contempt of court for punching a defendant, but…given what he said, I'll let it pass this once. But don't even think about doing it…*belch*…doing it again…*belch*…doggone you, Hank, what was in that stew?"

"Sorry, Judge!" Hank replied from somewhere in the crowd. "It was leftovers!"

"Left over from the war, no doubt." The judge put a hand to his belly and grimaced. "I'll deal with you later." He turned back to Ebba. "Let's proceed. Are you in fact what the defendant said you are?"

"Of course not! I would never do such a thing."

He looked at Daniel. "Have you evidence that this woman was, well, of a pure nature at the time you married her?"

Ebba watched Daniel's cheeks flush red. "She was untouched, if that's what ya mean."

The judge leaned forward and motioned Daniel to do the same. He lowered his voice and said, "Have you ever been with a woman before, son? Because if not, how would you know?"

"Beggin' your pardon, Yer Honor, but I have three older brothers, all married before I was. They made sure to fill me in on what to expect."

The judge sat back again and nodded. "Good point, son. You would know, then." He put a hand on the table and began to drum his fingers, then leaned forward to see if Stanley was still on the ground. "Someone want to toss some water on that boy?"

Deputy Turner nodded and went to find a bucket. Ma Weaver followed.

Everyone sat in silence as the judge continued to tap

the table. "Seems to me," he finally said, "we have a misunderstanding here. And being as how I have horrible indigestion, I'd like to wrap this up. My only remaining question is what gave Mr. Oliver…" He again checked on Stanley, who still hadn't stirred. "…the notion that this young woman was of, shall we say, ill repute?"

The room went silent as a tomb.

Judge Whipple studied Ebba a moment. "Miss, I think you look like a nice young woman, but one can't be too careful nowadays. It's also my understanding that this particular town doesn't have an active saloon that would employ the kind of women Mr. Oliver claims you to be. Still, did you do anything to provoke his actions?"

"No, Your Honor, I did not," Ebba said firmly.

"She didn't, but I know who did!" came a voice from the back of the room.

All heads turned as Clayton and Arlan entered, marching Nellie Davis between them. She was none too happy to be there, and certainly not happy to be there with the two men gripping her by the upper arms. Trailing behind was Mr. Davis, a stern look on his face.

"What's the meaning of this?" the judge asked.

"Why don't you ask Mrs. Davis here?" Clayton said.

"And why should I?"

"Because," said Arlan. "She took something that didn't belong to her and created a mountain out of a molehill."

The judge leaned forward and looked Nellie up and down. "Did she now?" he said. "Well, do tell."

Chapter Nineteen

"I did nothing!" Nellie spat. "Tell these two ruffians to unhand me!"

"Nellie," Mr. Davis warned. "Tell the judge what you did."

"You're not helping!" she snapped at him.

"I'm doing my best not to march you home and lock you up for the next six months! Maybe then you'll mind your own business!"

Judge Whipple leaned back in his chair, hands on his belly. "Make it quick."

"I'm guilty of nothing!" Nellie said, chin high.

"Mother, what have you done this time?" Charlotte groaned several rows back.

"She stole Daniel's letter from Ebba, that's what she did," Arlan told the judge.

"What?" Daniel turned to his older brother. "What she'd do that for?"

"Why don't you ask her?" Arlan said.

Daniel leaned past Arlan enough to look at Nellie. "Mrs. Davis, what is this all about?"

"I was doing my civil duty to protect your family from this…this…harlot!"

Daniel looked at Ebba, who was staring daggers at Nellie. "What is she talkin' about?"

Ebba shook her head. "I don't know. She's treated me strangely ever since I arrived."

"What was in that letter?" the judge asked Daniel.

"I can't say. I never really read it myself," Daniel said.

"Oh, illiterate, eh?" said the judge.

"No, Yer Honor, I can read fine. But my cousin Matty read it to me first, and then it disappeared. Or I thought it had." Now he was glaring at Nellie too.

"So what was in that letter?" the judge demanded. "I'm not gonna last much longer, son." To prove his point, his stomach began to make odd gurgling noises. Everyone backed up a step.

"I've got it right here." Mr. Davis pulled a folded sheet of paper from the inside pocket of his coat. "Seems my wife had hidden it in a drawer with her frillies."

"You went through my…?" Nellie began.

"One more word, dear, and I'll put you on a train back to Mississippi myself," her husband growled.

Shaken, Nellie went silent.

Someone else, however, did not. "Excuse me, Your Honor," Matthew said as he made his way to the front of the room. "I am Matthew Quinn—the 'cousin Matty' of which Daniel Weaver spoke. I am also Mrs. Davis's son-in-law. I did read the letter for Daniel when it first arrived, as he was too nervous to read it himself."

"All right," the judge said with a grimace. "And you're telling me this because…?"

Matthew shoved his spectacles up his nose as his cheeks turned pink. "The letter in question is of a private nature, Your Honor. I would not wish to embarrass my cousin's new bride by speaking the contents aloud. But as my mother-in-law read what I did, I can see how this got so out of hand."

Judge Whipple grimaced and gurgled once more. "Enough is enough! Give me the dangblasted letter and let me see for myself!"

Mr. Davis handed it over. The judge unfolded it and read silently, nodding a few times. When he reached the end, his eyebrows rose. "Hmmm." He slowly turned to look at Ebba, then sat back in his chair, sighed and looked at Daniel. "You should make it a habit of reading your mail, young man."

Daniel glared at Matthew. "I knew there was something Matty wasn't tellin' me, but I never got the chance to read it myself."

"And we know whose fault that was," Arlan said. "Don't we, Mrs. Davis?"

Nellie turned crimson, but said nothing.

"Wait a minute!" Ebba said. "Don't you think I know what I wrote to Daniel? I don't see what all this fuss is about! I never said anything in that letter that would indicate I was anything but who I am!"

The judge, along with every other man in the room, stared at her.

Ebba paled. "All I told him was…that I had all my teeth!"

The room erupted in laughter.

"Quiet!" the judge barked and rapped his gavel until the crowd shut up. He looked at Ebba. "Did anyone else have that letter before you sent it off?"

"No!" Then it hit her, and she put her hands on her temples. "Oh no…"

"Oh no what?" Daniel asked.

"Mrs. Pettigrew…she mailed it for me."

The judge's stomach rumbled. "Merciful heavens," he said with a grimace.

"Here, drink this!" Ma made her way through the crowd, a glass in her hand. "It's my own recipe. It'll help settle your gut, Judge."

Judge Whipple was in too much pain to argue. He grabbed the glass and downed the contents in a single swallow, then belched long and loud toward Nellie. "Oh my. Terribly sorry, ma'am."

"Great Scott, man!" Mr. Davis cried. "See a doctor!"

Ma wrinkled her nose, having been standing next to Nellie, but otherwise endured the onslaught stoically. Nellie still had her eyes closed.

The judge settled back in his chair. "Much obliged, ma'am. I feel better already." He looked around for a moment, his eyes finally settling on Mr. Davis. "I take it this isn't the first time your wife has done this sort of thing?"

"No, Your Honor, I'm afraid not."

"Your expression toward the woman at the moment would be proof enough, even had I not asked you," the judge said. "You realize the trouble she's caused this young lady?"

"Yes, Your Honor, I do."

The judge nodded, then looked at Daniel. "Son, I'd say you're a very lucky young man, but if I heard your bride right, she didn't write all of what's in the letter in question."

Daniel stood, dumbfounded. "What didn't she write?"

"See for yourself." The judge handed him the letter.

Daniel read it through, until he got to the bottom. "Oh. Well!" His face lit with a smile. "Shucks, that ain't no news to me!"

Ebba still had no idea what any of this was about. "Daniel, aren't you going to tell me?"

Daniel smiled at her. "Ah, sweetie, it ain't nothin' we don't already know 'bout each other."

"But what is it? Mrs. Pettigrew had to have written something in that letter before she sent it to you!"

Daniel smiled and showed her the letter. "She sure did."

Ebba looked…and her mouth dropped open. "What?" She turned to Daniel in shock.

"See? Nothin' wrong with that," he said. "I dunno why Nellie would take somethin' so simple and start a bunch of trouble about it."

The judge leaned over to look at Stanley, who was now conscious but had decided to stay on the ground for safety's sake. "Mr. Oliver, I find you guilty of attempted rape. I'm having you transported to McNeil Island where you will serve out a sentence of two years for your crime. And if I ever hear you've attacked a woman again, whether a 'soiled dove' or any other, I *will* make you wish you were dead. Is that clear, son?"

Stanley gulped. "But Yer Honor…"

"Is. That. Clear?"

"Y-y-yes, Yer Honor."

"Take this lowlife away," the judge told Tom Turner, who'd just arrived too late with the water.

Tom shrugged, set the bucket down, helped Stanley up and led him off to jail.

The judge turned to look at Nellie. "And as for the matter of Mrs. Davis and the rumors she concocted that started this whole mess…ma'am, I find you guilty of disturbing the peace. I sentence you to community service for a term of six months."

"Community service?" Nellie screeched. "You can't do that to me!"

"Make it nine months!" the judge said, then rapped his gavel on the table.

"But that's absurd!" Nellie shot back.

"*One year!* Or would you like to try for a year and a half?"

Nellie opened her mouth again only to have Mr. Davis clamp a hand over it. She struggled briefly, then glared at the judge.

Judge Whipple smiled. "Well, I'm glad that's settled. One year of community service, right here in this establishment."

Nellie's eyes popped as she shook her head as best she could.

"No, not that!" Hank cried from the back of the room. "Have some mercy!"

"Your stew didn't have any mercy on me," the judge said. "Putting up with her is the least you can do."

"Yeah, but this means we'll *all* have to put up with her!" someone said. Others laughed...until they realized what it meant to have Nellie working at Hank's for the next year.

"Well, I do need the help..." Hank said with a shrug.

"And Mrs. Davis clearly needs a dose of humility," Judge Whipple added. "Plus, look on the bright side, Hank—you won't have to pay her."

The place roared with laughter as Nellie stood in shock. She wanted to faint, but the men holding her wouldn't let her.

The judge smiled in satisfaction and banged his gavel once more. "Court is adjourned!"

"And do you, Harlan Hughes, take this woman to be your lawfully wedded wife?"

Harlan gave Mary's hands a squeeze. "I do."

The legal proceedings done, the Weavers had hurried to the church for Ma and Harlan's wedding. Clayton and Spencer tagged along after locking Stanley up. Tom hated to stay behind, but someone had to go over things with the judge and guard their prisoner.

"And do you, Mary Weaver, take this man to be your lawfully wedded husband?"

Ma gazed into Harlan's eyes. "I most certainly do."

Bella and Calvin's twins began to fuss, and each exchanged the baby in their arms for the other's. That quieted them for the moment as the preacher continued. "Then by the power vested in me by Almighty God and the Washington Territory, I now pronounce you husband and wife. Sheriff Hughes, you may kiss your bride."

"Simply Harlan will do, Preacher. I'm not going to be a sheriff anymore." He looked at Mary. "Being this woman's husband from now on is fine with me." He took her into his arms and kissed her.

A cheer went up, along with a few wails from the little ones, as the Weaver clan clapped and whistled their congratulations to the newlywed couple. "Way to go, Uncle Harlan!" Clayton said, slapping him on the back. "It's about time the two of you got hitched."

The congratulations continued as Ebba took Daniel's hand. "Thank you."

"For what, sweetie?"

"For marrying me."

Daniel turned her to face him. "Would there be a reason I wouldn't?"

"Maybe if you'd seen what Mrs. Pettigrew added to my letter, you'd have changed your mind."

"Are you kiddin'? That woulda made me want to marry ya all the more. To me, ya were just bein' honest."

"Except that it wasn't me."

"Don't much matter now, does it? We both know it's true."

She blushed. "Yes," she said as she locked eyes with his. "It is true."

Ignoring the bustle around them, Daniel kissed her. "I hope I helped make it true."

Ebba smiled against his lips. "You did."

"Ya did too," he whispered. "But promise me somethin'."

"What?"

"When it comes time for our younguns to marry, and if'n any of them sends away for a bride, promise me we'll read the letters they exchange?"

"Only if you promise that those letters never leave our house."

"I promise!"

"Good. Then I won't mind if any of our sons get themselves a mail-order bride."

Denver, Colorado,
1901

Fantine sat in shock. "You mean, all of that happened because of one little sentence you added to that letter?"

Mrs. Pettigrew nodded. "Some people are horrible gossips, *ma petite*. They should not be allowed loose on the streets!"

Fantine sat, her eyes still wide with shock. "But Mrs. Pettigrew. What *did* you write in that letter?"

"What does it matter? Everything turned out all right in the end. In fact, the Weavers have kept me in their confidence and entrusted me to send each Weaver son a fine mail-order bride. I have ensured they are all happily married these last twenty years."

"Twenty years? How so long? The oldest boy on the farm after Daniel was Alfonso was it not? And he was only fourteen in the story you just told me."

"Ah, but you forget about Rufi."

"But she is a girl, *Madame*. She would not send for a mail-order bride."

"No, but she sent for a mail-order husband!"

Fantine gasped. "There is such a thing?"

"But of course, *ma cherie*. I am a matchmaker, am I not? What does it matter if I have to send a man or a woman to a client?"

Fantine began to fan herself with a hand. "I have never heard of this before. How many men have you sent out to brides?"

"Not many, but I have done it."

"And the rest of the Weaver family, you matched them?"

"I am still matching them," she said, arching an eyebrow. "There are so many, and they just keep coming."

Fantine nodded. "They must be their own town by now."

"Not quite yet, as not all have remained on their farm in their lovely little valley. But there are enough."

Fantine smiled. "Please, *Madame*. Will you not tell me what you wrote in Ebba's letter?"

Mrs. Pettigrew sighed. "Oh very well, *ma belle*. I simply wrote this. "'I look forward to sharing a bed with you.'"

Fantine's mouth flopped open. "What? That's it?"

Mrs. Pettigrew nodded. "That's it."

"But…but…how could so much trouble be caused by such a simple statement?"

Mrs. Pettigrew smiled as she went to hang the letter back on the wall. "The heart, *mon agneau*, it governs our actions, does it not?"

Fantine slowly nodded her agreement. "Yes, I suppose it does."

"Well then, in the heart of an innocent, my simple statement brings joy. But in the heart of the wicked—in this case, a bored gossip—it lights the fires of contempt. For have you not heard the proverb, 'out of the abundance of the heart, the mouth speaks'?"

Fantine slowly stood. "I think I understand. But does that make the town of Nowhere wicked?"

"No, only the wagging tongue of one woman. In her mind, she thought she was doing good, but she wrought nothing but destruction. The Weavers have written to me with tales of Nellie Davis. She is not someone I would like to know, at least not back then. In Ebba's last letter to me, she says the woman has mended her ways. Too bad it took almost her whole life to do so."

"Yes," Fantine agreed. "Too bad." She looked at the dozens of framed letters on the walls. "Tell me about another bride."

Mrs. Pettigrew glanced around the room, went to the opposite wall and took a frame off its hook. "Ah, this one. Now this is a fine tale."

"What is it? Who is it about? Another Weaver?"

Mrs. Pettigrew smiled. "No, not a Weaver. A man named Eli Turner."

"Eli Turner? Who is that?"

"The younger brother of the Deputy Turner in the tale I just told you, the one who became the new sheriff in Clear Creek." Mrs. Pettigrew smiled in remembrance. "Now there is a town with some interesting people in it. A person could write a book. Many books, in fact."

"If they had, I would like to read them," Fantine said with a smile.

Mrs. Pettigrew looked at her. "Then you are in luck, *ma petite*. I have some of them on my shelves, written by Sheriff Tom Turner himself. You may borrow them if you like."

"Yes, I would like that very much."

Mrs. Pettigrew set the frame in her hand on the desk. "Now, let me explain your other duties."

"But will you not tell me the story of Eli Turner?"

"Not now—we have things to do. We are after all, first and foremost, matchmakers. If you are to be my assistant then I must teach you everything I know. So let us get started, shall we?"

Fantine smiled. "You mean… I have the job?"

"But of course, *ma cherie*. Now—to work!"

(Of that tale, anyway…)

* * * * *

WE HOPE YOU ENJOYED
THIS BOOK FROM

LOVE INSPIRED
INSPIRATIONAL ROMANCE

Uplifting stories of faith, forgiveness and hope.

Fall in love with stories where faith helps
guide you through life's challenges, and discover
the promise of a new beginning.

6 NEW BOOKS AVAILABLE EVERY MONTH!

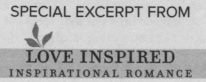
Clang, clang, clang.

The hammering outside her new schoolhouse grew
louder. Eva Coblentz moved to the window to locate
the source of the clatter. Across the road she saw a man
pounding on an ancient-looking piece of machinery with
steel wheels and a scoop-like nose on the front end.

When he had the sheet of metal shaped to fit the front
of the machine, he stood back to assess his work. He
knelt and hammered on the shovel-like nose three more
times. Satisfied, he gathered up his tools and started in
her direction.

She stepped back from the window. Was he coming to
the school? Why? Had he noticed her gawking? Perhaps
he only wanted to welcome the new teacher, although his
lack of a beard said he wasn't married.

She glanced around the room. Should she meet him
by the door? That seemed too eager. Her eyes settled on
the large desk at the front of the classroom. She should
look as if she was ready for the school year to start. A
professional attitude would put off any suggestion that
she was interested in meeting single men.

Eva hurried to the desk, pulled out the chair and sat down as the outside door opened. The chair tipped over backward, sending her flailing. Her head hit the wall with a painful thud as she slid to the floor. Stunned, she slowly opened her eyes to see the man leaning over the desk.

He had the most beautiful gray eyes she'd ever beheld. They were rimmed with thick, dark lashes in stark contrast to the mop of curly, dark red hair springing out from beneath his straw hat. Tiny sparks of light whirled around him.

"I'm Willis Gingrich. Local blacksmith." He squatted beside her. "Can you tell me your name?"

The warmth and strength of his hand on her skin sent a sizzle of awareness along her nerve endings. "I'm Eva Coblentz. I am the new teacher and I'm fine now."

Don't miss
The Amish Teacher's Dilemma
by USA TODAY *bestselling author Patricia Davids, available March 2020 wherever Love Inspired books and ebooks are sold.*

LoveInspired.com

LIEXP0220

"Don't look at me like that, April."

She raised her gaze to his. "Like what?"

His fingers tightened in her hair and her mouth ran dry. She swallowed. Moistened her lips.

She wasn't sure if she moved first. Or if it was him.

But then his mouth was on hers and like everything else about him, she felt engulfed by an inferno. Or maybe the burning was coming from inside her.

There was no way to know.

No reason to care.

Her hands slid up the granite chest, behind his neck, where his skin felt even hotter beneath her fingertips, and slipped through his thick hair, which was not hot, but instead felt cool and unexpectedly silky.

His arm around her tightened, his hand pressing her closer while his kiss deepened. Consuming. Exhilarating.

Her head was whirling, sounds roaring.

It was only a kiss.

But she was melting.

She was flying.

And then she realized the sounds weren't just inside her head.

Someone was laying on a horn.

She jerked back, her gaze skittering over Jed's as they both turned to peer through the curtain of white light shining over them.

"Mind getting at least one of these vehicles out of the way?" The shout was male and obviously amused.

"Oh for cryin'—" She exhaled. "That's my uncle Matthew," she told Jed, pushing him away. "And I'm sorry to say, but we are probably never going to live this down."

Don't miss
A Promise to Keep *by Allison Leigh,*
available March 2020 wherever
Harlequin Special Edition books and ebooks are sold.

Harlequin.com